Even Tears Are Good with Bread

FAITH RICCOMI

DEDICATION

First and foremost, to my precious Jesus: thank you for the gift of this story, and for teaching me endurance. This book is yours.

Special thanks to Dr. Paul Allison and Simon Parnham. You two read through various drafts of this novel and continued to encourage me forward. Thank you also to my students who read excerpts and kept telling me I had to persevere and publish it! You have inspired me countless time and in countless ways.

And thank you to Scott, my love, my *dragi*, who helped with the final edit.

But thanks most of all to my mom, who knows this novel inside-out and never stopped pushing me to finish it. You are more than my mom; you are my life-long friend, my mentor, my cheerleader, and my role-model. *Volim te.*

CONTENTS

NOTE

There is something you must realize before you read this book. If you are looking for the following pages to teach you great things about Croatia and its people, put this book down, and buy yourself a plane ticket. The novel you hold was not built upon great historical findings or fascinating anthropological studies. It is, quite simply, the perceptions of a young woman who grew up there; memories are faulty and slight impressions can become generalizations in one's mind.

As for the title of the book, it refers to a Croatian saying. In Croatia life revolves around bread; whether you're having breakfast, lunch, dinner, or a snack, you will find bread at the table. So as you read this book, stroll down to your local bakery and buy some nice, fresh bread and indulge. You might need some tissues too, but hey, even tears go with bread.

I

2000: Marko

Teacher was yelling at him again. Marko was trying to read better, but the words were long and complicated. He would focus so hard on reading clearly that by the end of each sentence he had not the smallest idea of what it all meant. At least he read better than Ante. That kid would stare at a word until the room seemed frozen and then force it out all choppy. Teacher never let Ante read more than a sentence.

As Teacher turned to another victim, Marko slumped down in his chair and swore under his breath like he had seen his *baka* do. Whenever someone said something she did not like, Baka would become even more hunched over inside her black clothes and mutter bad words. Mama just ignored her. She also ignored Marko when he swore—unless of course they were in public with her friends. Then she would yell at him and threaten some creative form of punishment, even though her friends often snickered to themselves.

Now Teacher was asking Tomo to read. Tomo, Tomo. Well, of course he started to talk about his chickens, the new coop he had set up with his grandfather, and… But Teacher gave him her mad look—or was her face permanently frozen in that frown?—and told him to read the paragraph in the book. Shifting in his chair and glancing to his right, Marko saw Maggie reading along in the book like he was supposed to be doing. *Ajme*, why was he stuck with the *Amerikanka*? She had been in classroom A with him since first grade, but now in fourth, they had to share a desk. Imagine, him sharing a desk with her. Since the beginning of the school year, about a month ago, the only thing she had muttered to him was not to put his books, pencils, or hands on her side of the desk. Girls.

Teacher was looking at her wristwatch again. A grin slowly spread across her face. "Ah, *marenda* time."

And with those two words, the metal chairs scraped against the scarred wooden floor as kids argued and pushed their way to the door.

Marko eagerly dug into the depths of his backpack for the paper bag that held his sandwich. He glanced over again at Maggie as she carefully picked through her own backpack for her snack. He had once watched a movie where an awful bell rang every time kids changed classes or went outside for play time. He wondered if that kind of obnoxious bell rang in the schools where Maggie came from. Grabbing his sandwich, he turned from her and hurried toward the door.

All twenty-seven students ran out the front door of the school and joined the dozens of other kids who were all bumping into one another. They either sat on the broken cement steps or leaned against the unpainted, concrete walls, quickly swallowing the little snacks their mamas had prepared them. Time was short with a lot to do in those thirty minutes.

As groups of kids finished their pastries or fruits or chips, they began their usual games. The girls went off to one side to play *lastrika*, a game Marko refused to even try to understand. What fun was it to jump over elastic? How could it compare to the thrill of kicking a black and white ball while sweating through the three layers Mama put on him, cursing at all the other boys and scoring a goal?! He rushed out to the cement court with the other fourth grade boys, eager to get there before the younger ones came begging to let them play. The little boys would soon learn that mercy was not to be found on a football court.

With no teachers, no difficult words, no girls, and certainly no *lastrika*, Marko focused on running, passing, kicking, and scoring. Over the years of playing together at school and in the streets, they had come to see him as a skilled player. They also knew his dad had been a great football player and respected Marko for that. He always had a spot on the court, regardless of the number of guys trying to play. Of course, that did not spare him from getting shoved or cussed at— hey, those were all part of the beauty of football.

When Marko scored the last goal before *marenda* ended, Ante and Dario slung their arms around his shoulders and sang proper football songs. They headed back to the steps as the day's champions. Laughing and talking with the guys, Marko glanced over and saw Maggie playing *lastrika* with all the girls. Matea and Petra seemed to be arguing over whose turn it was. Matea was saying it was hers, but Petra insisted it was Maggie's. As the two girls' voices grew more passionate, Maggie placed her hand on Petra's shoulder and quietly said she did not mind going after Matea. Petra muttered about Matea always getting her way, and Maggie gave her a smile and a quick hug before the game continued on. A teacher yelled at them to all come inside, and Marko groaned with Ante and Dario as they made their way back to class.

The last half of the school day was more yelling. Marko drew footballs next to his mathematics problems, wishing he could spend his hours on the cement court instead of in the smoke-filled classroom—he had counted: Teacher had gone through two packs of cigarettes since *marenda*. Now here was a proper mathematics problem: if Teacher smokes two packs on the second half of the day and one pack on the first half of the day, and five total on Fridays, how many packs does she smoke in a month? When 12:30 finally came, he and the other guys grabbed their backpacks and raced outside to play another game of football before they had to head home. Marko fought the wind that tried to tackle him as he flew back and forth between the two nets. Once again, he didn't have to think about history or math or the low mark he had received on the last science test. His focus narrowed: one more goal.

~~~

1997: Beth

"Mom, I don't get this."

Beth was trying to spoon pieces of apricot into baby Bruce's mouth. She never knew when he would actually chew the juicy chunks of apricot or throw them happily on the floor. When she succeeded in prying open his mouth and getting him to swallow a bite, she returned to stirring the tomato soup. "Sure, Maggs. What do you need help with?"

Maggie got up from the couch and shuffled over in her slippers to the kitchen table. Despite Beth's attempts that morning, Maggie's ginger curls ran wild about her face. At seven years old, Maggie should have been brushing her own hair but often didn't because her curls made it such a challenge. The next morning would be yet another battle with those tangles. Plopping a heavy, hardback textbook on the tablecloth, Maggie twirled her fingers through the pages. She placed her index finger on the right page and turned it around to face Beth. "This." She stood beside Beth, shifting from one foot to the other.

"Hmm…" Beth breathed in deeply and sat down at the table, motioning to Maggie to take a seat next to her. Maggie sat down, rested one elbow on the table, and cupped her chin with one hand—a common Maggie pose. As they stared together at the math question, Beth realized she needed some background knowledge. "Maggs, could you tell me about what you learned in class today so I can understand a bit better?"

Nudging some ginger curls out of her eyes, Maggie replied, "We learned about *oduzimanje*."

Had she heard that word before? Beth spooned another mouthful to Bruce, which he promptly spit back out. "OK, what's that mean?"

Maggie's face scrunched up. "I don't know."

Beth wiped off Bruce's mouth with his bib. Standing up from the table, she crossed the room and walked over to the door that lead to the hallway. A thick book propped it open so that the wind wouldn't blow it closed. Over the past few days, the wind had taken on a fierce chill, signaling that their fourth winter in Croatia was quickly approaching. Beth recalled Drew saying that the weather in Split was just like San Diego. Back when they lived in California, they often drove down to San Diego to spend family time at the beach. The weather seemed to always be perfect there: usually around seventies, not too cold and not too hot. While Split proved to have mostly warm weather throughout the year and hardly any snow, the winters brought a fierce, northeasterly wind called *bura*. She had even heard of a woman who had once been blown under a parked car. Wrapping herself tight in her wool sweater, Beth brought the large book to the table and turned toward the O section. Her eyes quickly scanned the words. *"Oduzimanje, oduzimanje...* oh, OK, it just means subtraction." Closing the book, she smiled at her little girl.

"OK..." Maggie raised her eyebrows. "Why is 'straction important?"

"Well, subtraction is..." Turning to Bruce, she tried to coax another spoonful of apricot between his laughing lips. This is just what she had been worried about. Back in 1993, when Drew came back from his visit to Croatia, she had expressed her concerns to him. He listened and they talked late into the nights with mugs filled with hot peppermint tea. Drew had convinced her that they should at least try and put Maggie into Croatian school. They had both agreed that they did not want her to be isolated; homeschooling her would only cut her off from everyone. They also did not want to portray that they thought their daughter too good for the Croatian public school system. It all had made sense then, but now with Maggie in first grade, looking up at her waiting for an answer, those concerns resurfaced. How could she help her daughter with her homework if she herself struggled with the language? She suddenly remembered that the soup was almost done, so she jumped back on her feet. Picking up the long spoon, she stirred the tomato bisque. "You see, Maggs, it's when you take one number and... it's like you have many things and then take some of those things away."

Maggie drew the textbook away from her mother and gently closed it. Then she leaned over to tickle Bruce. "When will Daddy be home?"

Drew was definitely better at this kind of thing. Trying to brush off the prick of Maggie's question, Beth pushed back a strand of hair from her own face. "Not for a while. He said for us to eat without him because he is at the church with

Pastor Tihomir and some other people for an important meeting."

"Why?"

"We're not sure…" Beth shook some salt into her hand and then tilted it, letting the crystals slowly fall into the pot. She rubbed her hands together to shake off any excess. "Pastor Tihomir didn't say what the reason for the meeting was."

Trying to edge a spoonful of apricot into Bruce's mouth, Maggie tilted her head to the side. "Maybe Pastor Tiho wants to plan an outing. We haven't had one in a long time." When Bruce opened his mouth wide and allowed the spoon in, Maggie laughed in victory then looked up. "Don't you love outings, Mom?"

Beth glanced at her daughter and leaned against the counter. "Yes. Yes, I do." Watching her two children laugh at one another, she pushed away the what-ifs and made herself stop looking toward the clock on the wall. "I tell you what, hon, let's call Tanja. Maybe we can ask if she can come after dinner and explain *oduzimanje* to us."

~ ~ ~

1993: Tihomir

"This is the highlight of Split."

Tihomir waved his hand over the boardwalk. Cafes littered the sidewalk leading to the edge of the Adriatic Sea. Husbands and wives laughed loudly with friends. Children wandered away from their parents and dangerously close to the water. Waiters meandered among the customers with a solemn look of "what do I care." Friends waved their hands dramatically as they talked and drank their coffees. With both hands on his waist, Tihomir glanced at Drew's face for a reaction. The American had just touched Croatian soil the previous night, and Tihomir struggled to tell what the quiet man was thinking. He slapped Drew on the back. "Follow me. The best way to know the people is to be among them."

Weaving his way between the tables, Tihomir found a small, round table with two chairs. He motioned for Drew to sit down. When the waiter came over, Tihomir ordered two coffees with cream for them. Yes, this American would soon discover the delicacy of Croatian coffee. "So tell me. What do you think so far?"

Drew lightly scratched his beard. "Seems like a lively... a pretty lively place. It wasn't what I expected, you know?"

Tihomir leaned a bit over the table and looked Drew in the eye. "Yes, a lively place, but filled with lost people." He lifted his right hand, palm up. "I once saw a Christian program of children from your country singing a song about God having the whole world in his hand." Tihomir pointed to the people walking by. "He holds every single one of these people inside his hand." He turned to Drew with a serious look. "Mr. Austin, they all have stories. When the war began two years ago, drugs came, crawled in and infected society. Our people, especially the young ones, you see—we lose their minds to the horrible needles." Tihomir reminded himself to take Drew to some of the alleys that were covered with heroin needles. He himself had hardly ever walked around the city without stepping on one.

"Our job is..." He reached into one hand and pretended to take something out. "...to take back what belongs to God."

The American looked at Tihomir's hands and then out at the people, his eyes squinting in the sun. "Such a beautiful place. A tourist wouldn't know the pain."

The waiter brought the two coffees. Lifting his own small cup to his mouth, Tihomir breathed in the sweet smell with his eyes peeking up to watch Drew's face. At six-foot-four, the American crouched over the cup and inhaled. He lifted it and drank a good sip or two, nodding and smiling.

Satisfied, Tihomir sipped and the two sat in silence, enjoying the breeze that brought relief against the sun. August continued in the heat of the summer and welcomed daily swims. Ever since Tihomir had moved to the coast, he had spent his summers at the beach. He was thinking that the next morning he, his wife, and Drew would all go for a swim before the day grew too hot. This morning Tihomir had gone swimming while the American had slept. He had never seen anyone sleep so long. Drew had described it as "jet lag," which sounded like what Croatians called *fjaka*, a word that described the laziness of the summer.

When he had finished his coffee, Tihomir set down his cup. Reaching into his shoulder bag, he pulled out a large, spiral drawing pad. To flip through it now in front of his new co-worker would be egotistical and inappropriate, but he wished he could just be a little boy and proudly show off his accomplishments. Only Zrinka took the time to admire his daily drawings, and she always had a fresh compliment. He now rifled through the bag for a moment before finding a pencil that would work. Then he began to sketch.

"I must tell you, Mr. Austin." Drew looked up from his coffee and watched Tihomir's hand decorate the blank page. "The church is small and without much oomph, you know? We must change this, but how?" He pushed the pencil's tip a bit harder to add depth and darkness. "They will not come to us in a building, not yet, so we must bring God to them." His fingers sped up with the pace of his words. "We must bring God here."

Tihomir set the notebook gently onto the table and pushed it toward Drew. He realized it was a rough drawing, but he had gotten down the basic lines of the boardwalk and a tall man on a platform with his index finger striking up into the air.

"Umm is that supposed to be me?" Drew pointed to the tall figure.

Looking beyond Drew, Tihomir set his eyes on the space he had modeled the drawing after. "Yes, tomorrow you will preach."

II

2000: Marko

The second he threw his backpack onto the hallway floor, he could smell lunch: bread, salad, tomato soup, *bread*, meat, spinach, potatoes, BREAD, and some cake leftover from the weekend. He peeked around the corner and saw Mama stirring this, tasting that... Ah, Mama was his favorite person in all of Croatia. Sneaking into the kitchen, he tore off a chunk of white bread before Mama could slap his hand. The crust crackled on his tongue as he tried to stuff another piece into his mouth, but Mama told him to get out of her kitchen, for God's sake.

Grabbing an old, deflated soccer ball, he chased it up and down the hallway. In between the two walls of chipped paint, he drew in a deep breath and found himself in a large stadium, perhaps in Munich, Germany. Thousands of fans were on their feet, yelling, singing, drinking. They were cheering for him, arguably the world's most talented football player. As he pressed toward the goal, their screams grew and pushed him forward as if their voices were a forceful wind and he a sail on the Adriatic. If only he had been paying attention to the player that had snuck up on his left side. He felt himself being crushed and then falling to the ground...

Mama picked herself up off the floor and gave him a good yelling. Hadn't she told him plenty of times not to play football in her house? She brushed herself off and told him to stay out of her way. When he went to hug her with a big grin on his face, she suppressed her own smile with more scolding. She swatted at him and told him to wash his hands because lunch was ready. Then she asked Marko to go wake Baka from her nap. He kicked the football past her and her scolding and down the hall of the apartment. When he reached the second door on his left, he slowly opened it. Baka swore at him as he let some light into her dark room. Baka, Baka—she was always either sleeping or spitting criticism on someone. Her voice was so ugly because she had smoked three packs every day since she was Marko's age. But she was not completely horrible. Sometimes she snuck him coins to buy something sweet or smiled at him with the few teeth she had left. And when she was in an especially good mood, she would pat him on the head and say, "You are a good boy."

Marko went over to her bed and allowed her to lean on him as she slowly sat up and then stood up. With her arm in his, Baka shuffled and grumbled her way to the table. Mama continued to hasten around the kitchen, cutting more bread, filling the bowls with soup, until Baka muttered for her to calm herself and sit for one moment. When all three were seated, they touched their foreheads, chest, and both shoulders quickly, muttering to Marija and some saint to bless the food. While Marko worshipped the meal with enormous bites, Mama and Baka chewed a little, then talked about how Stipe—the fat midget of a man who owned the bakery—was seen with three different women that week—what could they want with him except to get a few free pastries—and the priest's daughter—what a little whore—she would be there tomorrow at mass completely drunk—and that loner man down the road—what was his name again—he was spending all his money on cigarettes—not that there was anything wrong with cigarettes—and the American family—what heathens."

Marko paused the spoon in front of his mouth. Heathens? He took the bite, focusing his eyes on his plate and his ears on the gossip.

Mama stabbed some spinach with her fork. "They have been here for how many years, and they have never come to mass? Not once, you know? And they don't pray to Mary—that's what I've heard. I bet they don't even celebrate Christmas."

Baka grunted in agreement. "They always have people over at their house, doing God-knows-what. They're a cult, I tell you."

"Zdenko, their landlord, he told me that they don't do anything. They sit around the house every day, drinking coffee, talking to people, as if they had nothing better to do. How does the woman have time to clean?" Leaning forward, Mama confided, "And Zdenko told me that they get their money from other Americans." She slapped the table with her hand. "People just hand over checks so they can come to our country while I work at the grocery store all morning, come home and cook lunch, and then go to work for another nine hours. Why are they even here? We don't need their help." She threw her hands up in the air, which was Mama's sign that she had said all that needed to be said.

While Mama and Baka bantered on about the bad economy and low paying jobs, Marko put a slice of meat between two pieces of bread and opened his mouth as big as he could. Heathens. Maggie might say 'hello' instead of 'halo,' and she might be a bit quieter sometimes than the other girls, but she didn't seem like a horrible person. She didn't celebrate Christmas? That was practically a sin, wasn't it? He shifted in the wooden chair and wondered how he felt about sharing a desk with a *heathen*.

~~~

1997: Beth

Shutting off the light, Beth turned when she heard Maggie whisper, "Mom."

"Yes, hon, what is it?"

From the light of the hallway, she saw Maggie motion to her with her little hand. Beth came and sat back down on the bed. "What's wrong?"

Maggie shifted in her bed, pulling the sheets up to her nose. Even in the dim light, Beth could see the fear in her daughter's eyes. "Maggs?"

"I told Petra today that we are missionaries."

Beth's eyes felt wide and large. "What?"

Maggie covered her face with her hands. Her voice sounded muffled. "We were walking home and Petra asked me why we were here in Croatia. I was so excited to finally tell someone, so I said we were missionaries."

"Maggie, we're not supposed to tell people that." Beth smoothed out some wrinkles on Maggie's sheets. "Croatians become really offended at people coming to be missionaries to their country. They go to church and they believe in God, so they often think that we should go to other places where people don't believe in God at all. "

"But, Mom, she's my best friend. Best friends tell each other their secrets, right?" Maggie looked up at the ceiling.

"When I told her we were missionaries, she said she had to go home, and she left before I could tell her goodbye."

Beth wanted to yell at Maggie. Even though Croatia was not necessarily a dangerous place for missionaries as far as persecution, the neighborhood might ostracize them, or the government might kick them out. "Maggie, you have to be more careful."

"You don't understand." She turned over onto her right side, away from Beth.

Beth rubbed the back of her own tight neck. She looked out the window in the corner of the room where a lamppost lit the darkness outside, and the wind beat against the trees and the houses. Every now and then, an eerie sound that Beth hated—the sound of cats fighting—pierced the quiet and took away any sense of peace. Leaning forward, Beth whispered, "Maggs." She tapped on the small form in front of her. "Maggs, look at me."

Maggie rolled back over, her eyes distant and solemn.

"I'm sorry. Today was a hard day for you. And I'm sorry Petra reacted the way she did. But you know what, sweetie?" Beth rubbed one of Maggie's curls between her fingers. "Petra is your friend. When someone is your friend, they stick close to you no matter what. I think if you talk to her, she'll understand."

Maggie wiped her nose with the back of her hand, and Beth handed her a tissue from the nightstand. "You mean that if I tell her the whole story of how God told us to come here, she might understand?"

"No." Beth let out a raw laugh. "No. I think you should explain to her that we work for a humanitarian organization, helping people."

"You mean lie?"

"No, it's not lying. We do work for a humanitarian organization. Remember the times we've gone to the refugee camps, given people food, and given kids toys?" Maggie nodded. "We help people who need it."

"But it's hard to say. Humanit…" She shook her curly head. "Missionaries is easier."

"Well, we'll just practice saying it so it'll be easier. But listen to me carefully, Maggs." Beth paused until she had her daughter's eye contact. "Don't tell people we're missionaries, OK?"

Maggie's face was scrunched up, but she answered quietly, "OK."

"Good girl. Now give me some hugs." Beth lifted Maggie up into her arms. "It's going to be okiday, Maggs. Everything will turn out all right with Petra." Beth held Maggie close, stroking the ginger tangles that curled about the little one's face. She could feel her daughter's trust pressing into her own chest. With eyes closed, together mother and daughter breathed and hoped.

~~~

1993: Tihomir

Tihomir slumped down into the couch and let out a deep breath. "*Ajme*, I am tired." With a giant yawn, he propped up his feet on the coffee table.

Drew joined him by crumpling into one of the chairs in the living room. Throughout the past week, the American had made himself at home in Tihomir's small apartment. He spent the nights in Tihomir's office on a makeshift bed Zrinka had set up for him. And every day he ate up anything Zrinka made: stuffed peppers, sausage, fish stew, crepes… He said that when he returned to America, his wife would be shocked by all the weight he had put on. Tihomir had grinned and said that they would take care of that by all the walking they would be doing. Why Americans drove everywhere was a mystery to Tihomir. Why drive when you could walk? Tihomir was glad, however, that Drew was enjoying the food so much. The more Drew was able to enjoy of Croatia, the more likely he was to stay. And no one could feed a hungry man like Zrinka. Even now, she entered the living room and handed them both a hot cup of coffee. She also placed a plate of fresh cookies on the coffee table. How she could serve alongside him in ministry and then cook elaborate, delicious meals for him and guests would always bring him amazement.

Zrinka sat down next to Tihomir, her shoulder touching his. After a long day, it was good to be able to sit next to her and be close to her. She had no idea how her gentle, feminine presence could cause his heaviness to wane away. Cradling the small white coffee cup in his hands, Tihomir took a sip of the hot liquid. "I believe today was very successful."

Leaning into him, Zrinka spoke, "I am so happy. Many people come close to Drew while he speak. Very quick, the group grow very big. People walk down to market, and they stop to find what the man with translator is say."

Drew brought the coffee up to his nose, inhaled long and deep, and smiled. "Thank you for the coffee, Zrinka."

She nodded to him. "No problem."

Drew took a sip and set his cup down. "Yeah, Tanja did an incredible job translating. She kept up with my pace and didn't miss a beat. "

Tihomir laughed. "And that one time when you said Peter instead of Paul, she caught what you were trying to say and made the correction without a single hesitation."

"So I was told." Drew laughed. Leaning back in his chair, he laced his fingers behind his head. "I was so nervous, wondering what I would say, but the words just, I don't know, came. I've never experienced God working through me like that." He shook his head. "It was like watching a miracle happen. And it was almost like I wasn't a part of it. I just got to watch it happen." His eyebrows bunched together. "Does that even make sense?"

Tihomir laughed lightly. "Yes, my friend, it does." Intertwining his fingers with Zrinka's, he studied the pattern their hands formed as one. He had been crazy nervous as a teenager when he first took her hand. Now it was as if it was a part of himself, belonging to him. He looked up. "God is a crazy one, and I am excited to see what he will do next."

Drew leaned even further back in his chair and closed his eyes. "Mm, so what is next?"

Zrinka looked up at Tihomir. He took another sip of coffee and then said, "I say let's take a couple days off evangelism."

Drew smiled. "Sounds good to me."

"I would like to take you up north." Tihomir squeezed Zrinka's hand. She knew how he had been longing for a trip up there.

"Why up north?"

"It is where my family lives. I would like you to meet them. I think you will like them, especially Mama. My mama is a great cook."

With eyes still closed, Drew's smile grew wider. "Sounds real good to me."

~~~

"We are almost there." Tihomir tried not to grip the wheel with excitement—Drew would think he was a little child. Although he was a bit nervous about the safety of the drive, he was excited to show Drew around the house of his childhood as well as eat some good lamb off the spit. The American had not yet tasted *real* Croatian food.

Drew switched on the radio and twisted the knob around until he came to the station they had been checking every once in awhile throughout their fifteen-hour trip. Tihomir glanced over at him. "Relax, *okej?*" Tihomir reclined in his seat as if he was not worried at all. "I have come up here several times a year and never had to worry about war trouble too much. I am sure we will get there without any problems."

Drew nodded. "Right, yeah… Yeah, we'll be fine." He slouched down into his seat and propped his elbow on the armrest.

Tihomir could not wait to get out and stretch his legs. This car was cramping both of them—he and Drew were close in height, with Drew standing only a few centimeters taller. And this car had not been made for people with long legs. The poor little white Yugo was a small car that would hopefully get them up north and back without breaking down. Glancing over at Drew, Tihomir thought about how some people had commented that they looked almost like brothers. With both of them standing tall with curly, dark hair, they also both had a nice dark shade to their skin. Though neither had grown up directly on the coast, they both had spent many summers at the beach. Drew's family had driven down to San Diego, and Tihomir's mama had loved taking her children down south to the beaches of Split. Every summer she would pick four of them, five if they squished, to go in the car for the long ride down to the coast. They always went in the last week of the sixth month, right after school got out. All of that month they would try their hardest to please her: helping her make soup, killing the chickens for dinner, and other tasks they usually left up to her.

As soon as they got into the car and their spot in the car assured, they would begin yelling, throwing stuff, and hitting one another. Once the trip had begun, sainthood was over. To prolong her sanity, Mama would stop every couple hours down the coast so she could visit with some of her friends and get some food for herself and each of the kids. She would sip coffee and ignore them completely while her friends would talk about the village idiot who got some girl pregnant again. Mama would listen intently, shaking her head at the atrocities and exclaiming *"Bože sad cuvaj"* every few minutes.

On the way up north, Tihomir and Drew stopped at the same places so Tihomir could introduce the American to his people. He knew that the more people Drew met on his trip, the more he would feel connected to Croatia in general and the more he would want to come back to stay for a long time. Tihomir hoped Drew would not come for just a year or two like most missionaries he had heard of.

Looking over at Drew, Tihomir observed the thoughts bouncing around in the man's eyes. Focusing back on the road, Tihomir thought about how he was still trying to figure out the American. Drew did not say much but always held the expression of much thinking going on. Tihomir turned right onto a smaller road. "I have confusion about your work in America. You work with computers, right?"

Drew shifted toward Tihomir a bit. "Yeah, I work in artificial intelligence, helping computers work kind of the way minds do."

The car bumped around on the dirt road. Timor grinned. "Ah, but you cannot make a machine work like one of these." He pointed to his head.

Sitting up straighter, Drew responded, "Obviously we can't create exactly what God has done with our minds. Far too intricate." He shifted a bit to face Tihomir. "But we can mimic some aspects of the brain's actions and transfer them over to a computer program."

"Hmm very interesting." Tihomir tried to process what the American had just said to him. He had a computer at home, but that black box of a thing did not seem to have near the potential of the human mind. Before he could ask more questions, he saw a sign on the side of the road. "Ah, here we are!" He pointed to the white sign with black lettering: *Zeleno Polje*. "This is my village."

The American studied the sign. "What does it mean?"

"Green Field."

"I see." Drew sat forward in his seat and seemed to observe and absorb every detail he saw outside the window.

Green fields spread out everywhere the two men looked. Small houses lined either side of the road, each one closely connected to each other. Gardens decorated the fronts and sides of the houses with every kind of vegetable one could imagine: potatoes, cabbage, zucchini, carrots... Tihomir grinned. Home.

With a turning of the wheel, Tihomir maneuvered his car left and up beside the house where he had grown up. He honked the horn, and soon people came piling out of the house with yells and shouts and *ajme*s.

Mama reached him first when he came out of the car. She kissed him forcefully on both cheeks. Waving her hands all over the place, she spoke loudly and as if in a hurry to say everything at once. In the midst of her talking, her grin loved him, bringing back flashes and hints of memories of a hard childhood that she had managed to make a bit beautiful. She kissed him again. Then when she pulled back from him, she became completely silent, and therefore, so did everyone else. They had noticed the awkward man who still stood beside the car with one hand in his jeans' pocket. Mama walked toward him with her head cocked like a puppy. She seemed to be studying him, trying to decide if she would like this foreigner. Then, decision made, she burst into the same ritual of kissing him and talking to him. She spoke just as loudly but a little slower as she struggled to say the English words in the right way. When she stumbled, she would exclaim "I so sorry!" And Drew would smile big and wide and nod at her to go on. Tihomir could tell: the American liked her.

One of his younger brothers, Neno, came over to Tihomir and kissed him on both cheeks and asked him how life was down in Split. While they talked, they grabbed the two bags from the backseat and brought them into the house. Mama had her arm looped through Drew's as she told him to call her Bosiljka. She nodded with encouragement as Drew tried a few times to pronounce it. When he said it just right, she clapped her hands and kissed him on both cheeks again.

As soon as they walked into the house, everyone took off their shoes and put on some slippers. Mama found a dark blue pair and handed them to Drew. Tihomir grabbed one of Neno's pairs and slipped them on. He carried his bag into his old room, which he would once again share with Neno and their other brother, Hrvoje. Both in their twenties, Neno and Hrvoje lived at home as everyone waited for the two of them to get married. They, on the other hand, seemed content at the moment to simply have many girlfriends. Tihomir went over to Janja and Visnja's old room, where Neno had dropped off Drew's bag. Janja and Visnja had already married and moved into their husbands' houses so that now their room was vacant. Glancing around the room, Tihomir stood with his hands on his hips and asked Neno about the plans for this upper floor.

His brother stood in the middle of the room, spreading out his hands and explaining. This floor would have belonged to Tihomir as he was the oldest, but he had moved down the coast to Split. Now it would go to Neno. Once Hrvoje found a girl, the family would then help him build a new house next door. Neno told Tihomir how they would make their old room into the kitchen and living room and make Janja and Visnja's room into the big sleeping room. The bathroom would remain the same. He shrugged and said that it would not be a hard task at all; he simply had to install a kitchen. Now all he had to do was find a girl. He slapped Tihomir on the back and commented that perhaps he should drive down and get a girl from the south, as Tihomir had. The two brothers continued to talk and laugh as they left the room to rejoin the rest of the family downstairs. Following Neno, Tihomir paused for a moment at the top of the stairs. To his right, the door was still closed to a small room. As he had done countless times over the years, he pressed his hand to the door.

Precious Ana.

III

1997: Beth

Beth wiped the counter with a wet rag. "I don't think we should worry too much about it."

Drew slurped another spoonful of soup. "What if Petra tells her parents?" He stared down at the bowl.

Beth smirked. "Maybe the whole neighborhood would find out and we'd be on a plane back to Sacramento."

Looking up, Drew stared at her, eyes wide, eyes that said, *How could you even joke about that?*

Turning away from him, Beth rung out the rag. While talking to Maggie, she had been concerned, but now with Drew, she didn't want to take it so seriously. "There's nothing we can do about it now." She lay the rag over the faucet and turned around, with a smile. "So let's talk about something else. Like…" She laughed. "I almost forgot to tell you what Bruce did today. He was…" Looking up at Drew, she trailed off. His eyes were on her but almost as if viewing a stranger. As his eyebrows drew down in confusion, her grin slipped off her face. She stood there, her hands aching for a task, something to release her from his gaze. "Would you like more soup?"

"Beth."

She reached for his bowl and brought it back to the stove. "Some of the ladies at church say you're too skinny. You really should try to eat at least a little more."

"Bethy."

She paused in front of the stove, and her shoulder lowered. Bethy. She smiled. His nickname for her. She had been twenty-six when she first met Drew, and they had been friends for years before they dated. Their favorite thing to do was go on long bike rides. He would race ahead of her and say, "Bet you can't ride faster than me, Little Bethy!" She was actually four years older than he was, but at six-four, he was definitely the bigger one of the two of them. She would then yell back to him, "You're about to meet your match, Big Dave!" Then she would pump her legs hard until she laughed her way past him. Time would get lost somewhere after the first mile as they rode up and down the streets of Sacramento's outskirts.

Now he stood, came up behind her, and circled his arms around her waist. He held her there, breathing against her neck, for a few moments. Then he turned her around, grasped her hand in his, and led her back to the table. His hands pressed lightly on her shoulders, coaxing her to sit down. Then, without any plea from her, he began to knead worries down from her neck to her shoulders to her arms until they filtered out from her fingertips.

She laid her head on the table and let him rub her shoulders with his large, strong hands. She let out all that she felt about how she could not help Maggie with her homework, how after four years her pronunciation still broadcasted her American nationality, and how the cashier at the store had laughed at her bad grammar when she was paying for the groceries that day. "You and the kids can all speak decently well, but with my Michigan accent, people struggle to understand me."

With his palms flat, Drew smoothed out her back, and she felt more of the tension release. "You know, that's the first thing I noticed about you." She could hear it in his voice—that one-sided grin. "I thought you were so cute with your little Midwest ways."

She lifted her head just enough so she could glare up at him. He leaned down and kissed her, despite her attempt to be miffed at him.

Laughing, he pulled back a bit, studied her eyes, and gently put a loose curl back in its place behind her ear. "You will get it. You will. People learn at different speeds." He paused. "You know, yesterday I was thinking—Tanja needs to make some extra money. How about if you set up an hour or two a week to meet with her? She might be able to help you through some of what you've been struggling with." He took her hands, brought them up to his lips, and kissed them lightly. "You've been working so hard on your own, trying to keep up with the language as well as with the kids. Now that we have Maggie in school and Bruce is taking naps more regularly, it's time to focus on what you need."

A private tutor. Someone to guide her. "That would be—it'd be wonderful. But... but can we afford it?"

He shrugged his shoulders. "We'll find a way." He had that glow in his eyes—the problem-fixer had struck gold.

Now she took his hands in hers to kiss them. Then she paused and groaned. "Ah, I'm so sorry. I didn't even ask you about the meeting. How did it go?"

Drew breathed in roughly and looked up at the ceiling. "As good as it could go."

Tracing the lines on the palm of his hand, she asked softly, "What did Tihomir want?"

Drew stared at their hands together and lightly shook his head. "He…"

She watched her husband as he transformed from a strong man who laid away all his worries and stresses so he could focus on hers to a crumpled, defeated looking man. Watching him made her feel helpless, and she struggled to keep quiet until he spoke.

His voice was soft and broken. "He had all the people on leadership there. And he asked them, one by one, to say what they thought was wrong with me—how I had failed them."

No, he wouldn't. Tihomir had his issues, but he wasn't a cruel man. There must have been some misunderstanding.

He fingered a loose string on the rim of the frayed tablecloth. "Then, when that was over, Tihomir asked me to quietly leave the building and respectfully keep away."

Picnics, laughter, dozens of conversations, late nights at each other's houses—two couples who shared everything. Beth held her husband as he cried. He, the strong one. She attempted to offer him some kind of reassurance. At the same time, she brainstormed what to do when Sunday came, and Maggie wanted to pick out a dress to wear to church.

~~~

2000: Marko

Mama tugged Marko down the isle, determined to get to *their* pew. Throughout Marko's whole life, the three of them, once the four of them, had sat in the fourth pew on the left side. It had been his father's favorite pew, and Mama did not like to change the way Tata had done things. She shoved and pushed out of her way—as gently as a Croatian mama could—every child, teenager, and grieving widow. Marko though he heard Mama mutter something about what the church really needed was for Moses to come back and part the seas of this crazy congregation. After conquering the crowd, Mama proudly claimed her seat and beckoned for Marko and Baka to quickly sit down. The organ music had started, signaling everyone to stop gossiping and have a seat. After the first song faded, the priest came up and began to sing his chant in a muttering monotone. At the appropriate places, Marko muttered back the appropriate phrases. The nun who taught his catechism class was forever making each of them repeat these prayers over and over again. He had not the smallest idea what any of it meant, except that he would one day go to heaven because of the prayers, and that seemed a good enough reason for him.

Halfway through all the muttering, Marko heard footsteps. Oh-ho-ho, someone was coming in late. He turned to his right, slightly so that Mama would not notice and then swat at him. She said that it was disrespectful to look back while praying, but what could one do when curiosity beckoned? He turned a little more so that he could get a better look.

Maggie?

Slowly, more people turned to look until half the congregation was staring at the American family's entrance into the church. Even the priest stumbled a bit in his words as he looked up at them before focusing his attention back on the book of prayers in front of him. Marko thought about what must be going through everyone's minds—he had heard Mama and Baka say before that the Americans often frequented Dobrislav's grocery store, and they also bought fresh bread every other morning from Josko's bakery. But throughout the past seven years in which they had lived in this neighborhood, the American family had never stepped inside the church.

As most everyone watched, Maggie's father walked confidently with one hand on his wife's back and the other holding the chubby hand of a small boy. Marko was pretty sure that the boy's name was something like Brusi or Bruko. Watching the family as they searched for an empty pew, Marko thought about what Mama and Baka had said the other day—he did not think that these people looked like horrible *heathens*, whatever that meant. Each of them had a pleasing look about them, especially Maggie's mom who smiled around at every face she saw with the big American smile: starting in the perfect, white teeth and transferring over to the shining eyes—just like the movie stars, just like Julia Roberts.

And Maggie, who walked beside her mother, well, her eyes seemed to be everywhere. Marko glanced around to see what she was looking at. The various paintings of Mary and Jesus on the walls. The ceiling that looked so far away. The curtain that marked confession. She walked down the aisle with her family, and then as she passed the fourth pew, her eyes drifted to Marko's face. His own eyes jumped down to his shoes, and he twisted around on the wooden pew. He couldn't understand. Had Mama not said that these heathens did not go to mass? Why were they here then?

Since the church was well-filled, the family had to sit in the front row, and everyone peeked at the back of the American heads throughout the rest of the service. Toward the end, Mama whispered across Marko to Baka, "Are they going to take communion?" Baka shook her head, muttered some word she should not have, and then both she and Mama quickly crossed themselves. Marko wondered the same as they waited. When the time came for communion, he stood up and followed Mama and Baka to the front of the church. He had only recently had his first communion, and it still made him nervous. He realized how simple it was, but he could never remember whether he was supposed to stretch out his right hand to receive the bread and use his left hand to put it into his mouth, or if it was the other way around. He was positive that he would one day get it wrong, the priest would yell at him, and Marko would be banished from the church and have to convert to Orthodox or some other abominable religion.

Since they sat down in the front pew, all four Americans were some of the first to go up to the priest. Maggie's father led the way with the little boy in his arms. Marko heard behind him a few coughs and not-so-quiet-objections. When Maggie's father came up to the priest, Marko half expected the priest to refuse to give the American the bread, perhaps even tell them to leave. The whole church seemed to take in a big breath and watch quietly. For a moment, the priest stared at the family and did not move, but then he made the sign of the cross over the tall man just like he did with everyone else. When the father and mother had taken communion, Marko glanced at Maggie's face. It was red, and her eyes were stuck on the floor. Marko had this awful feeling inside and did not like it, so he tried to ignore her and focus instead on the bread the priest was about to place in his mouth. If only Marko could take the communion plate and eat the whole loaf by himself. One bite was mere temptation, not enough to satisfy. He was sure that was blasphemy, but still… bread was one of God's greatest gifts to humans, at least to Croatians, was it not? As Marko accepted the bread from the priest, he wondered whether he could be both a famous football player and a famous baker. He returned to his place in the pew and thought about the possibility. Surely he would make a lot of money. Football and bread—what else did a man need in life?

~~~

1993: Tihomir

Rubbing his eyes open, Tihomir wondered at first where he was. Then he glanced to his right and saw Neno and Hrvoje's sleeping forms.

Home.

Diving his feet into the warm slippers, he stood up, stretched, and yawned loudly. Shuffling over to the other side of his bed, he blinked until the fog passed. The window in front of him framed the outside, and with nothing moving, it looked like the perfect painting. The artist had painted a seemingly endless spread of fields, speckling them with the greenest of greens, deep shades of brown mixed with lighter shades, and hints of yellow. He longed to jump into the painting and run without any inhibition, his hands and legs pumping and the wind resisting against him. He faintly remembered his dream last night which he was almost sure included some kind of running. When he was just about to grasp onto a fragment of the dream, it crumbled before him and left him staring at the fields.

A run would feel good today if he could make it outside before it grew too hot under the summer sun.

When Tihomir crept down the stairs, he found Drew looking at the sole photograph on the hallway wall. Tihomir went up to him and nodded upwards at him. "You slept well?"

Drew nodded. "You?"

Opening his mouth wide in a yawn, Tihomir nodded. From the way he felt, it seemed like he had disappeared into a deep sleep for a few months. He wished he could remember the dream though.

He was about to walk toward the kitchen when Drew pointed to the yellowed picture. "Is that your dad?"

The picture had been taken when Tihomir was five years old, so his two younger sisters were not in the picture. No one was smiling, as was fairly typical then. His father, who stood at the back of the picture with a hand on Mama's shoulder, was tall and had a slight stomach. "Yes, that's him."

He could sense the question Drew wanted to ask, but Tihomir did not want to answer it. Today was a day to enjoy. He clapped Drew on the back and said, "Come, friend. I am sure my mother has breakfast ready for us." Sure enough, that very moment Mama yelled out for everyone to come eat.

Everyone crowded into the kitchen, yelling at one another. Observing all the pushing and shouting from his spot against the wall, Drew leaned over and said to Tihomir loudly so he could be heard above the clamoring, "Are they always this mad at each other?"

Yelling at his cousin and then reaching for some bread from the counter, Tihomir tilted his head at the American. "What do you mean?"

Drew motioned around the room. "They're all yelling at each other."

Tihomir laughed. "My friend, yelling does not mean anger, not always. This is normal. We talk loud when we're happy, angry, sad, excited, any big emotion, you know?"

With a grin, Drew followed Tihomir's example of grabbing a couple slices of bread from the table. Tihomir showed him the various spreads he could apply to the slices: butter, nutella, and many jams. He explained to Drew that everything was homemade by the people of the village, except for the nutella, of course, which came from the nearest grocery store a half an hour away.

After most everyone had sat down around the table and in various chairs set up around the room, Mama went around to her children and some other relatives who had popped in for some breakfast. She made sure each person had enough bread and spreads. While everyone was yelling and eating, Tihomir's uncle shouted across the room to one of Tihomir's older cousins. The room began to breathe deeply of laughter as the cousin made a mad face and shouted back at the uncle. From his spot at the left side of the table, Drew watched the comments bounce back and forth with energy. Tihomir leaned over. "Darko asked Ante how he has gotten so fat."

Drew turned to Tihomir. "No wonder he's angry."

Tihomir waved his hand. "Ah, he's not really angry. It is not so bad to say here to say that someone is fat. When I was in your country, everyone is very—sensitive, yes? Here we say what we think, and it's *okej.*"

"Don't people get offended?"

Tihomir shrugged. "Yes, but—." He laughed. "I don't know. It is not so bad."

Mama came over to Drew with a huge smile, placing more bread on the American's small plate. Tihomir leaned back in his chair with his mouth full and chewed with contentment. Even with the war going on, Mama made sure everyone had more than enough to eat. She had an almost magical way of making food spread far. He glanced around the room, noticing the torn clothes that he knew his family had worn for days without washing. Drew and Tihomir had brought some clothes they had received from a humanitarian organization with a plan to distribute the clothes later on in the afternoon. He glanced over at Mama and then to Tihomir and his clothing. The American wore a striped blue and black shirt with khaki shorts. No holes. No faded colors. Tihomir wondered—would this man care enough to get his hands dirty, care enough to stay? From the grin on Drew's face, Tihomir began to hope.

~~~

Later that night Tihomir tried for a half an hour to keep his eyes closed; he just wanted to sleep. Neno and Hrvoje were out drinking with their friends and would not be back for a few hours. *Ajme*. Tihomir shifted in his bed, but turning over onto his right side did no good. Breathing in deeply and letting the breath out slowly achieved nothing. Last night he had fallen asleep almost right away and slept deeply, but tonight he only felt the ache in his shins from his four-mile long run that day. He also was more aware of how much he missed Zrinka's body next to his. She didn't have to say anything; just her being there, breathing alongside him, coaxed him into sleep.

Shifting his pillow, he decided to brainstorm about his sermon for the following Sunday. Bringing his arms behind his head, he stared up at the ceiling. He could talk about Paul. Yes, he could talk about Paul's conversion, his ministry, and his letters to the churches while in prison. After all, Paul was a good, no, the perfect example of a godly man who followed Christ's teaching relentlessly.

Unlike himself.

Tihomir turned back onto his left side. No, he would not think about that now. Paul. He needed to focus on Paul.

When preaching, Tihomir could read the verse in Philippians 3—he was pretty sure it was verse nine, or was it ten?—the verse that talked about God calling people righteous because of their faith.

Was Tihomir righteous? Did he have enough faith? How could he know whether his faith was strong enough, of the right kind, of the right depth, for God to declare him righteous?

Feeling the pressure build up inside his chest, Tihomir wished Zrinka had come with them. She would sing to him in a low, melting voice, and he would forget his failures and worries. When she was around, he was able to see God in her, and he was comforted, but without her, he did not seem to be able to find God in the dark. God liked Zrinka. Well, who did not like her? Everyone at church spoke to her about their concerns and asked her for advice or prayer. Even the people at the cash register at *Konzum* would find themselves telling her silly little details about their day because she had those eyes that listened and a posture that breathed patience. When at home, she would pray for the people whose names she had written down, often praying the words of a given passage from her worn Bible.

Tihomir pushed the sheets off his body and stood up to switch on the light. Unzipping his backpack, he reached in and took out his wrinkled, discolored Bible. The Psalms were usually more comforting to him than other parts of Scripture, so he turned to where he had left off the night before: Psalm 110. After reading through the verses, nothing really stood out to him or moved him in any way, so he continued on to 111. Verse 1: "Praise the Lord." Tihomir sat on his bed, staring at the words, willing himself to obey the command to praise God. Lifting his hands, he tried singing quietly one of the worship songs that spoke of praise. He had sung it loudly and full-heartedly last Sunday. Now the words seemed meaningless and pointless, so he lowered his hands. He tried to think of things he could be thankful for. He and Drew had gotten to Zeleno Polje safely, hadn't they? That was something to thank God for. But had God done that? Or had it just been a safe day to travel? What if they had not gotten there safely? What if the Serbian army had attacked their car? Would God still be "good"?

He shut the Bible and set it on the floor. He was too tired for theological, philosophical questions. Pulling the sheets in around him, he decided to leave the light on. Darkness would only intensify the what-ifs.

IV

2000: Marko

Marko opened his eyes, and the world was just as black. No moon out tonight. He lifted his head to peer out his window. Clouds seemed to be hiding even the stars. This was darkness.

He laid his head back down, closing his eyes once more. Nights like this, he could not tell if he had fallen asleep at all. He felt like he had been lying there for an eternity. Had he dreamed? He had vague remembrances of some kind of dream—something about a tree with sap crawling up its back? His dreams were always strange. Turning over onto his side, he licked his dry lips and thought about how much he hated sleeping. He could be doing countless other things: eating, playing football, joking around with friends, drawing… Why, he would even rather be in school and be yelled at by Teacher than just lay here like a dead fish.

Lightning filled the room and startled him. He sat back up and waited, counting. Four seconds later thunder rocked his bed and rumbled in his chest. He grinned and pushed off his sheets. Swinging over to place his feet on the floor, he began tiptoeing quietly to the door. Pushing down upon the handle ever so slowly and ever so gently, he crept out of his room like a soldier creeping up upon the enemy. His father had taught him how to walk so that not even the keenest of ears would be able to catch him. Marko had used this skill to scare Mama many times. On his toes, he avoided certain parts of the wood floor that he knew would give him away. With his hands on the wall next to him, he felt his way down the hallway. Now and again, lighting would light up the house, and he could see where he was. When he reached the living room, he carefully pushed down on the handle of the glass balcony door. He stepped out, closed the door behind him, and sucked in the cold, wet air. The wind blew rain onto his face, his hands, his chest.

His father had brought him out here many times. Whenever there was a thunderstorm, Tata would sneak into Marko's room and motion to quietly follow him. The first time had been when Marko was three years old. After several times, Marko would hear the thunder and meet Tata out in the hallway. They would steal out to the balcony and stand with their hands on their hips and their faces to the sky. This was a time for them to demonstrate their fearlessness. The lightning would beam out her quiet strength, the thunder would bark out his defiance, and the two humans would bask in the rain. The simple act of standing in the rain, taking whatever it threatened, seemed to indicate a "Give me your best shot" attitude. At times, he and Tata would look at each other and begin to laugh. And how Tata could laugh. Deep, loud, no holding back. The time for tiptoeing past, Tata let all depth break loose from within him. Marko would laugh alongside him, trying to conjure up the kind of depth Tata did.

Marko now tried again, but his voice still had not sunk down into his chest. He had noticed in class that some boys, like Tomo and Ante, would have this sort of crack in their voices. How humiliating. He hoped to avoid any cracking and go straight to the deep-down-in-chest sound.

The rain began to fade to a mist, and the thunder grew softer. He was drenched, his pajamas sticking to his skin and his normally curly hair flat against his head. Yet he knew Mama would not yell at him the next morning. Every time he did this, she would quietly ask him to take off his wet clothes. She would bundle them up, wring them out over the balcony, and hang them out on the clothesline. The first time he had been so startled by the quiet of her reaction that he watched her from the living room, wondering why she was not scolding him for doing something so foolish. He had watched as she pinched his shirt with two clothespins and then looked up to the sky. She had shaken her head with the slightest of smiles and a look, a special kind of look. For days afterward, he had tried to remember where he had seen that look before. That look seemed to say a great deal, as if some sort of secret, or multiple secrets, lay hidden inside of it. Then he had realized that she used to give Tata that same look. They would be having dinner or would be talking in the living room, and in the midst of the conversations and everything, Tata would look at her, and she would look back at him.

It was a look of knowing. A look of love.

~ ~ ~

1997: Beth
Beth felt Drew squeeze her hand. Side by side, they strolled down the Riva, the ever-popular boardwalk of downtown Split. Taking their time, they were on their way to a restaurant

they had yet to try: Maslina. The name meant "olive," which made sense considering all the olive trees that sprinkled the Croatian landscape. Zrinka had recommended the restaurant, emphasizing that the cook made his own bread. Croatians prized their fresh, tasty bread, and any restaurant that served bought bread was an embarrassment.

She smiled up at Drew's tall frame and walked closer to him. They hardly ever went out to dinner in Croatia, what with two children, a church, and various ministries to attend to. Beth promised herself that she would not worry about any of those things. Tonight she was not the mother, the missionary, or the pastor's wife—she was simply Beth.

They had chosen to go to a restaurant in the heart of Split. One of the largest cities of Croatia, Split certainly came alive at night. Every mother, child, teenager, and old man was out on the town. Couples walked hand-in-hand, teasing each other and offering little kisses here and there. Parents yelled loudly at their children as the little ones ran about screaming and laughing. People popped in and out of little stores that lined the main walkway, looking for name brand clothing, whether they could afford it or not.

Beth looked down at her simple dark blue dress. She had bought it at Target for under twenty dollars last time she was in California. Back in Sacramento, she had enjoyed shopping at Nordstrom and Ann Taylor. But when packing to come to Croatia as a missionary, she had thought that she would need to dress simply. This dress was one of the few "nice" outfits she had brought. When talking about what she would wear with Zrinka, her friend had tried to persuade her to buy a new pair of shoes to go with her dress. Croatians would easily whip out 300 kunas, around $50, for a pair of shoes. And that was their decision. But how could she justify spending that much on shoes when she was a missionary? Her old black pumps would do just fine for tonight.

When they arrived at the restaurant, Drew took her coat, hung it up on a rack by the door, and then pulled out her chair with a smile. It reminded her of their first date, when he had tried to pull out her chair for her at the last second, causing her to lose her balance and land clumsily on the floor. His mortified face and constant apologizing had made her smile, and as he helped her up, she decided that she would go out again if he asked. She could tell now that Drew was remembering the same instance, for his mouth widened knowingly.

When the waiter brought them their menus, they spoke to him in Croatian with their American accents. He switched to English, as people often did with them. Beth ignored him and continued in Croatian, ordering for herself a Fanta with ice. He of course looked at her strangely when she mentioned the ice, but she did not care. Slightly cool, almost warm drinks had never appealed to her, and tonight she wanted ice.

When the waiter had left them, Drew did that thing where he moved his lips to say something and then lightly shook his head. Beth moved a strand of hair out of her face. "What?" she asked.

He leaned forward and took her hand in his, rubbing her wedding ring. "Nothing, Bethy." He lifted her hand up to his lips. "You look beautiful."

Looking down at the cloth napkin she had spread across her lap, Beth felt her cheeks grow warm as they often did when he complimented her. "Thank you." She looked up at his face, which grew tanner every summer they spent in Croatia. "Not looking so bad yourself."

His eyes tiptoed across her face. He was tracing her. Once she had asked him why he did that, and he had replied, "I'm taking your picture, memorizing your face in this moment." She had told him to just get a camera since that would probably make her feel less awkward, but he had only laughed and told her to relax and let him enjoy her beauty.

Beth looked around them and noticed that the restaurant wasn't too crowded. More people were at the bar than at the tables. The room was dimly lit, and some traditional folk music played lightly on the speakers above their heads.

Drew spoke up, "We should go shopping afterward."

Beth tilted her head. "Why?"

"Why not? You could get some new clothes."

"I don't need any new clothes."

"But you've hardly bought any clothes from Croatia."

Beth smoothed out the napkin that lay in her lap. Had he been in any of the shops? Everything was much more expensive in Croatia.

Drew rubbed his chin. "I just thought you might like to spend a little money on yourself for a change."

"It's not very practical."

"Life doesn't always have to be about practicality. I like it when you spend money on yourself and dress up."

Beth pulled back her hand from Drew's. "We're missionaries, Drew."

He cocked his head. "So? Beth, being a missionary doesn't mean we can't enjoy any pleasures in life."

"Well, maybe I just don't want to waste money like people do here."

Leaning forward, Drew lowered his voice. "Come on, Beth, don't talk like that here. What if someone hears you?"

Beth crossed her arms and looked across the room at another couple. They were drinking wine and sitting close to one another—no arguing or shouting. She closed her eyes. When Mom and Dad had argued, she would hop on her baby blue Schwinn bike, pedal down the sidewalk, and picture herself riding down the coast of southern California. One day she would move far away from the Great Lakes and venture off to the great Pacific Ocean. She opened her eyes.

No escape.

"Beth…"

Her smile—yes, she needed to find her smile. Act like everything was fine, just fine. Wherever they went, they were representing Christ. The Messiah wouldn't argue, would he? Here in Croatia, they had to be especially careful.

Back in Sacramento, the two of them would drive down to Old Sacramento and pop into the variety of shops. He would tease her, and she would feign annoyance. They would go to the bookstore and read to each other for hours, and she would laugh at the voices and accents he would come up with. Then they would wander over to an ice cream shop and people watch. They would comment on the madly-in-love couples, the children who were high on sugar, the old man who carried countless stories in his wrinkled face… They enjoyed sitting and watching other people's lives walk past them. Now they were the ones being watched. As missionaries, they were ever on a stage, expected to mess up at any moment and then get booed off. Beth wondered at which unexpected moment it would happen.

The waiter came up to them and gave them their drinks. Beth ordered a chicken pasta dish, and Drew ordered the "mixed" pizza: ham, cheese, and mushrooms. After the waiter left them, the two of them leaned back in their chairs.

Drew fiddled with some toothpicks that were stored in a small container on the table. Beth quietly said something about going to the restroom and slipped away from the table. Once inside the tiny bathroom, she looked up at the mirror. That face—that tired and worried face—reminded her of someone. She leaned in and peered at the eyes that stared back at her. Yes, it was the face of her mother.

~~~

1993: Tihomir

Grinning in anticipation, Tihomir watched Mama finish her preparations for lunch. She had arranged salad on small plates and was popping in and out, as she had a light tomato soup on the inside stove and breaded chicken on the stone oven outside. He was a lucky man: Mama was the best cook in northern Croatia, and Zrinka was the best in the southern portion. He looked at his belly and patted it with a nod of his head. "You see, my friend, I am blessed."

Drew patted his own stomach. "I've been very blessed since I've come here." They were both standing in the doorway, watching Mama cook since she had chased them out of her kitchen with a wooden spoon. Tihomir remembered the times he would sneak into the kitchen for a piece of bread, and Mama would hit his bottom with the big spoon. But it had been worth it. Mama's bread was better than any bakery's because she made it *ispod peka*. Drew had asked him earlier what that meant, so Tihomir had explained how Mama would build a fire on a big stone until it became really hot. Then she would put the fire out and sweep the ashes off. She would place the dough on the stone, a dome over the dough, and the ashes and some cabbage leaves on top of the dome. This would keep in the heat, and the bread would be done and delicious in about half an hour. Drew had been stunned by the size of the loaf, practically the size of a car wheel. The American seemed enchanted by the taste of the bread and ate several pieces at each meal.

Mama now called out for people to come eat the food. Drew and Tihomir ran to the table and grinned at Mama's shaking head. She said something about boys never growing up. For lunch, the three of them were joined by Tihomir's brothers and grandmother. Baka stumbled in, muttering about everyone being too loud for her old ears. Tihomir and his brothers leaned toward her and said things like "Ah, Baka, you sweet thing, how happy I am to see you!" She would swat them away and hide her smile with a distinct frown.

Mama was trying to yell above all the other voices, serving them all first a cucumber and tomato salad. She filled each of their white bowls, engaging in small conversations as she moved about the room. Just when she had finished, the front door to the house was slammed shut. Everyone continued eating with their heads down. They kept talking, though somewhat less lively. Drew's head had popped up from his plate, his eyebrows scrunched up and turned toward the door. Tihomir hunched his shoulders over his plate and concentrated on forking the vegetables of his salad into his mouth.

"Where the hell is my food?"

Tihomir had known that *he* would appear at some point. *He* always ruined things. He ruined meals, football games, laughing conversations with Mama, play times with friends—everything. Even now, he strode over to Mama, who was still serving people, and laid a tight grip on her shoulder. He muttered in her ear, immediately causing her to set the bowl of salad on the counter and get a plate out of a cupboard.

Once she had layered his plate with vegetables, he looked at Tihomir's brothers, and the two of them promptly scooted their chairs to make room for him. He sat down and began to gently place bits of his salad into his mouth. He had always been such a careful eater, taking his time and eating one small bite at a time. While chewing, he looked up at Drew and said in Croatian, "Who is this son of bitch?"

Mama gasped from the counter and looked full of worry at Drew as if he would get up and leave her house right at that moment. Drew, thank God, was looking around at everyone, his eyes searching for a clue as to what was being said. Tihomir swallowed a bite of his salad and pointed his fork toward Drew, "This son of a bitch is Drew."

Mama came up softly behind her husband. "Miro, Drew is visiting from America with Tihomir. He will maybe come back with his family and stay for a year or so."

Miro smiled, looked at Drew, and spoke to him in immaculate English. "Ah, yes, Americans are huge benefactors to Croatian pastors, particularly ones who cannot properly provide for their flock."

Drew raised his eyebrows. Clasping his hands together, he leaned forward. "Well, my hope is to aid Tihomir in any way that I can."

Slapping the table, Miro laughed hard and caused Baka to jump. She had been eating silently without paying much attention to the talk at the table. Now she glared up at him, and he apologized to her with a charming smile. Then he looked at Tihomir while continuing to speak to Drew. "This little pastor can use all the help he can get."

Drew glanced at Tihomir. "Well, sir, I think your son is an excellent leader and certainly has a passion for God and people." He picked up a piece of bread and ripped it in half. "But tell me, what do you do for a living?"

Miro stared at Tihomir with a smirk. "Has he not told you?"

Tihomir stared right back at him.

Drew answered, "No, sir, not yet."

Taking another bite of his salad, Miro chewed it slowly, swallowed, and responded, "I'm a pastor."

V

2000: Marko

Marko stood with his right foot balanced on a metal can, pretending that he had just received a ball from another player. Backing up, he eyed the goalie. Then, running back up to the ball, he kicked it and watched as it spun in the air. It flew toward the net, barely missed the goalie's extended hands, and the crowd deafened Marko with their loyal applause. He fell to his knees, crossed himself, and let out a cry of victory, his teammates rushing toward him with their own shouts of triumph. Yes, Marko Kovacic would prove to the universe that Croatia had the best football team.

Oh to play in the FIFA World Cup.

Continuing down the road, he glanced up and saw a man coming out of a house. Marko tried to remember his name. He believed the couple's last name was something like Milic, and this had to be the husband. Marko had not seen him often, as *Gospodin* Milic did not come to mass. Mama and Baka had talked about this northern man who had moved into *their* neighborhood, God-knows-why. *Gospodin* Milic had not come from the village of Poljica like the rest of them. What was he thinking bringing his wife here? At least she was from southern Croatia, or Dalmatia as they called it, and the couple did have a Dalmatian dog. Did that count?

Marko's father had once told him the story behind the Dalmatian dog. When Marko was really young, maybe four years old, his dad was sitting on the couch, taking a nap in his camouflage clothes. Marko had whispered, "Tata." His father opened one eye and mumbled a "what." Marko shuffled over and asked Tata why the spotted dog was called a Dalmatian. His father wiped his eyes and mouth with his hand and began to tell the story of how a long, long time ago gypsies had come with wagons to Dalmatia. To protect themselves, these gypsies had strangely spotted dogs that would watch over them. The Dalmatian people saw how protective these dogs were and decided to have them guard the city during times of war. The dogs were named after the region and continued to help take care of the people. Marko asked if Tata worked alongside any Dalmatian dogs in the war, and his father had laughed. Tata had always had the best, deep laugh.

"Marko!" A voice brought him back to reality. Marko's friend Tomo waved to him from across the street with the biggest, silliest grin on his face. Marko sighed and crossed the street. Tomo motioned with his hands for Marko to follow him to his front yard where a large chicken coop stood. A rooster and a bunch of hens were shrieking and pushing each other around. Marko shifted from one foot to the other as Tomo talked about the new hen his grandfather had bought to produce more eggs. All Marko could smell was poop. He was nodding along with what Tomo was saying when Tomo's father came out of the house.

The big bellied man looked at Marko and then back at Tomo. "Shut up, you stupid boy. You don't see your friend does not want to hear all this?" Tomo dropped his head.

Waving his hands about, the man preached down to his son. "All day you sit out here and talk to those pathetic birds. You're supposed to be out playing football, like a normal boy, like your friend here." He pointed to Marko.

Shifting his feet, Marko tried to think of something to say, a way to leave.

Tomo's father continued, "You won't get any friends talking like a fool to these feathered idiots. I tell you, if it were up to me, I'd sell all these chickens."

Tomo's head shot up, but he kept silent.

His father began to walk away, kicking a chicken out of his path, cursing at it. Marko noticed that the man's eyes seemed to hide behind a shiny covering. Beneath the film, they shifted constantly, as if searching for something. Marko wanted to leave, to go far from those eyes.

The man was saying something, but with his back to them, it was difficult to understand his words. He trailed off as he shuffled out into the street and down toward the small grocery store.

The two boys stood there, watching the chickens squawk at each other. Tomo cleared his throat, but his voice still cracked when he spoke. "I think the chickens want to be left alone now. Too much attention for one day... I'll see you tomorrow." And he walked inside his house, shutting the door behind him.

Marko had that same awful feeling as he had had when Maggie's face had gone all red at mass. Glad to leave the stinky chickens, he turned away from the coop and walked down the street. He saw Tomo's father inside the store on the other side of the street, probably getting some more beer or cigarettes. Kicking a small rock down the road, Marko headed toward home and thought about Tata's laugh.

~ ~ ~

1997: Beth

Beth helped Maggie with her sweater and coat. The seven-year-old had to bundle up tightly for school. Although it usually took Maggie but fifteen minutes to get to the school, the harsh *bura* today would make it a fiercely cold walk. And when she did arrive, the school was not well-heated. At least she had a good teacher who made sure the kids were all as comfortable as possible, sometimes meaning that they kept their coats on throughout the day.

"Think you'll be warm enough?"

Maggie's little voice came out muffled. "Mom, I can hardly move or talk."

Loosening the scarf, Beth smiled. "I think you'll be just fine." Her daughter's eyes peeked out beneath all the clothes surrounding them. A hazel color, her eyes changed depending on what she was wearing, and right now the fluffy, green hat was bringing out a vibrant green in her eyes. Beth reached out and brushed the curls out of her little one's face. "I love you, Maggs."

Maggie seemed to hesitate. Then she wrapped her arms around Beth's waist. "Love you too, Mom." Then she turned around and hobbled down the hallway and out the door.

Hearing a little giggle, Beth turned back toward the kitchen, where Bruce was crawling about. When she saw him, she yelled, "No!"

There was Bruce with the biggest smile on his face, lifting up his hands toward her. His hands were covered in egg yolk. Their fridge was a small square box that was perfect for his crawling height, and, unfortunately, he had recently learned how to open it. The day before, Beth had bought eggs and had placed them in the individual crevices meant for the them. Now the fridge door was wide open, and eggs covered the rug. It was a brand new rug from Biserka, a woman from church, who had given it to Beth only a few days prior. With a smile as big as Texas, the old woman had extended the rug toward Beth and explained how she had been wanting to give the family something, make something for them, ever since she began coming to the church. She was elated to finally express her appreciation of them. Beth was not a crier, but that gift had almost caused her eyes to gloss over.

Now she was upset that Bruce had ruined such a lovely gift. "No, Bruce. Bad, that's very bad." She took a rag from underneath the sink, wet it, and began to wipe off some of the yolk from his hands. He had managed to also smear some of it onto his face. He was still laughing, apparently proud of his accomplishment. Beth tried hard to maintain the stern, Mom-is-mad look. He batted at her face with his sticky hands. "Ew, no, Bruce, stop it." He just gazed up at her and kept giggling. Gritting her teeth together, she let her arms collapse into her lap. She looked at the little chubby face with his mouth wide open in pure glee and his eyes wanting her to enjoy this moment with him. The anger slipped down from her face, and she burst into laughter. She leaned forward, attacking him with tickling. He bopped around, chuckling with a sort of old man laugh and saying little baby words only the depths of her could understand. When she sat back criss-cross-applesauce on the egged rug, he climbed up into her lap and began to spread yolk onto her sweatshirt. Rubbing her nose against his, she let him touch her face with eggy hands. It was as if he was blessing her, baptizing her. She accepted the blessing.

They sat like that, playing, and giggling with one another until the doorbell rang. Bruce had started to stand up, and the doorbell startled him. He fell back and hit his head against the tile. "Oh, honey." She grimaced as he let out a wail. Scooping him up, she whispered little words of comfort as she went to the door.

Upon opening the door, she saw her dearest friend. "Zrinka! Come in, come in."

After hugging and kissing Beth, Zrinka asked what was wrong with Bruce. Beth explained. Zrinka began talking in Croatian to Bruce, gently brushing his thin hair off his forehead. With his bottom lip protruding, Bruce spread his arms out toward Zrinka. Beth protested that he was far too messy, but her friend just laughed, took Bruce into her arms willingly, and rocked him lightly. Shuffling over toward the couch, she sat down with him in her arms, humming to him and tracing his face with her finger. Beth smiled; she had seen this many times. Whenever children were hurt or crying, Zrinka would take them and speak tenderly to them. They would gaze at her and seem to slowly forget their problems. She would sing some Croatian folk song to them in a soft, quiet voice, as she was doing now with Bruce. Then she would whisper a short prayer in their ear and with an amen, kiss their cheek. It worked like magic. Bruce, like all children, had after only a few minutes calmed down and was sucking on his index and middle finger, as he often did when he was relaxed and content.

"You have such a way with children."

Zrinka smiled down at Bruce, rocking him in her arms. Kissing his forehead, she whispered something in his ear. Then she turned and looked up at Beth. "So you must tell me. How was your date last night?"

Beth sat down next to Zrinka and Bruce. Wiping some crumbs off the couch, she answered, "It was all right."

She did not have to look up to know her friend was watching her, waiting for more. Zrinka had a quiet persistence about her. She never pushed, only waited. Even with all that had gone on between their husbands, Zrinka still knew Beth better than most people did.

"We had a bit of an argument." Beth leaned back into the folds of the couch. "I got upset, as I always do, just like my parents did."

Zrinka shifted Bruce in her arms. "Does this scare you?"

"A little." Beth played with her wedding ring. "I don't want to fight like they did. Always yelling, blaming…"

"You are not your mom, Beth."

Rubbing her forehead, Beth said, "I know. I just… I don't want to make the same mistakes as she did."

Zrinka leaned over and with her free hand squeezed Beth's hand. "I will pray for you. But remember: do not worry. Worry will eat you like those stupid rabbits that eat the lettuce from my garden."

Beth squeezed back with a small smile. The two of them talked about Maggie and how she was doing in school. Beth was about to ask Zrinka a question about Maggie's homework when the front door banged open. Both of them jumped. They glanced at each other and then down the hallway. The footsteps were hard and heavy.

Tihomir.

He stood with his hands on his hips.

"Zrinka." He motioned toward her. "Come now."

With her head down, Zrinka responded in an almost silent voice, "I came to visit my friend."

He strode toward her, took Bruce from her hands, and handed him to Beth. "I said come now."

Bruce had started crying again, louder and harder than before. Zrinka looked at Beth and softly said, "I am sorry." She stood up and followed Tihomir out the door.

Beth stared at the back of the door, holding Bruce tightly to her chest, lightly shushing him and telling him that it was OK. She tried to sing the song Zrinka had been singing to him. Forgetting some of the words and trying to swallow down the anger that kept rising within her, she struggled through the song, and Bruce continued to cry.

~~~

1993: Tihomir

Extending his hand toward the water, Tihomir explained to Drew. "This is our river, the Drava."

The two men stood side-by-side on the edge of the river. Trees and plants crowded in among them, yellow flowers ruffling themselves up against their legs. The wind pulled at the men's hair and clothes, drawing them in toward the water. Looking down, they saw their reflections mingled with that of the surrounding mountains and clouds.

This was Tihomir's sanctuary.

He sat down on the grass and dirt and pulled out of his bag a drawing pad. Flipping open to a fresh white page, he took a charcoal pencil to it and began to fall deeply into each line. He did not copy mere images onto the paper. He drew what he felt, what the Drava spoke to him, what it said about the God he could not understand in other places, man-made places that lacked this holy simplicity of nature. Why did they hold church in a building? How often those four walls crowded him and made him wonder and wander.

Drew crouched down next to Tihomir and looked at his drawing from a distance in a non-intrusive way. His eyes took in the shadings without judgment, and Tihomir felt free to let the pencil run across the page without much thought. He would not let the perfection that continually stalked him interrupt this communion with God.

After drafting several sketches, Tihomir laid the book aside and gazed down at the Drava. He could interrupt the silence with only a whisper: "She is beautiful, yes?"

Drew was sitting with his elbows resting on his knees. "Yes."

Tihomir pointed to the right. "Farther down that way she will meet up with the Danube. You have heard of this river?"

Drew nodded.

"When I was little, I ran here every day after school and drew, leaving homework for later. It was then Drava began speaking truth to me."

Holding a piece of grass in his hands, Drew broke it in half. "What does she say?"

"She says, 'No, no.' " He waved his pointer finger. "Do not worry, my friend. Do not bring troubles into this sacred meeting." He waved his hand about to represent the current. "To fight my current is to miss my beauty. Let it go. Let all of *It* go... Just be."

Drew studied a small rock, smoothing over it with his thumb. "What is *It* for you?" He tossed the rock into the river.

Biting down on his lip, Tihomir threw one rock, then two, into Drava's hands. *It* began to weigh back down on his chest. He found a round rock and threw it sideways, causing the rock to skip three or four times. Tihomir interlaced his fingers and then spoke. "*It* means whatever question is on my mind that day, sometimes it can be more than one."

"I take it that it's not a question like 'why do pigs not fly?'"

Tihomir gave one of those dark laughs that made him feel heavier. "Ha, no, much harder questions that our dear God is…" He tilted his head toward the cloud-spotted sky. "… slow to answer."

Drew looked out at Drava. "Does she ever answer the questions?"

Tihomir watched Drava slip over the rocks, smoothing them with her tender caresses. "No, that is not her job. Well, she… she does not directly answer them, but sometimes she helps me in different ways that make these questions seem less… heavy." He lowered his shoulders. "She lightens where others add weight."

"Others… like your dad?"

A cloud had been inching toward the sun and now covered it, dimming the lights on the men.

"I'm sorry. That kind of slipped out." Drew waved his hands about. "I've just been curious with the picture and lunch today." Drew's words sped up. "I know I sometimes ask the wrong things or say the wrong things. You know, my mom was always after me and now my wife—I just need to learn to reign it all in rather than, you know, spitting it all out onto people."

Tihomir slapped Drew on the back. "My friend, you don't talk much but when you do, it is like you are throwing out all the food you eat up."

Drew shook his head and laughed. "Yes, I suppose it's kind of like that."

Tihomir stood up and walked closer to Drava's edge. "But you are right in wanting to know. I am sorry I did not explain until now, but he is someone people do not talk a lot about, you understand."

"He's a pastor?"

"He preaches, and they call him pastor, so I guess yes, he is."

Drew twirled a piece of grass around in his hand. "Does he act like that in church, I mean, the way he did at lunch?"

Tihomir looked down at the American. "Of course not. They all think he is a very godly and wise man. He has a way of preaching, with emotion and passion." He kicked a rock into the water. "They think his words are from God Himself."

Drew's eyebrows knit together. "But he treats you all like dirt."

Looking down, Tihomir pressed his foot down into the ground. "Yes. Dirt."

VI

2000: Marko

Marko walked silently beside Mama and Baka, his head down. The car ride there had taken a while since so many people were going to Lovrinac that day. It was, after all, the Day of the Dead. Some people called it All Saints Day, which never made sense to Marko. Why would they go to the cemetery on a day that celebrated saints? Many good people were buried there in those graves, but Marko did not think they were considered saints.

Mama stopped to buy two bouquets of flowers from one of the women, all of whom were muttering and rasping out their advertisements to the people walking by. Then the three of them entered the cemetery with Marko shuffling behind Mama and Baka as they made their way down the pebbled path. When they arrived at the gravesite of the Kovacic family, Mama handed Baka one of the bouquets, and the old woman laid the flowers down on the grave with shaky hands. Lately her whole body had been shaking, just like Teacher's finger did in class every day. Baka's cough had been getting worse, and she looked as though a bit of *bura* would send her flying off. Marko now laid his hand on her shoulder, as if to hold her down.

Mama then placed the other bouquet on the same grave. Here father and grandfather were buried, along with other relatives. What Marko didn't understand was why Tata and Dida needed flowers. For the love of Mary, why would a guy ever want flowers? Tata had been a strong soldier, a football player, a man—it was bad enough that some men had to give women flowers. But receive them?

Mama and Baka rocked back and forth, letting tears out with slight moans.

Marko did not want his cheeks to shine with wet like the women. He was a man, after all. With a glance to his right, he saw a man with crutches standing in front of a grave. The man did not have a left leg, just one side of his pants scrunched up around the stump. He didn't seem old—he didn't have grey hair or wrinkled skin, but he was hunched over with eyes fixed on the grave in front of him. The man didn't move, just stared, as if waiting for something to happen. Marko looked back at his father's grave as rain began to trickle down and turn the ground dark. He was glad Tata had not come back from the war with only one leg and eyes that always stared.

~~~

When they came home and the rain had stopped, Marko decided to sit outside, right in front of the house. After a few minutes, Mama came down and made him stand up until she put a cushion down for him to sit on. It was a warm day, but Marko tried not to talk back to Mama on days like today since she was usually crying or angry or fussing over someone.

Throughout the hours following their visits to the cemetery, he just kept quiet and let her do what she needed to.

After Mama left him, he pulled out a rosary from his pocket and tried to remember a prayer from his catechism class. Maybe he could pray for his father. But memorizing the prayers never came easily to him, and right now he could only come up with pieces.

When he heard his name being called, Marko looked up and saw Tomo walking over. That kid had the funniest way of walking. Now that Marko thought about it, it was kind of the way a chicken walked.

Tomo kicked a ball to him. Picking it up, Marko twirled it around in his hands and then tossed it back to Tomo.

"You want to play?"

Marko shook his head.

Tomo cocked his head. "Why not?"

"It is the Day of the Dead. It would not be respectful."

"Oh yeah, I forgot."

Marko had never seen Tomo or his family at Lovrinac. He knew Tomo had a grandfather who had died in the war. Tomo would sometimes tell stories about what a great man his grandfather was and how he fought valiantly in the war. But when Marko had asked Mama, she had said that the family never visited the cemetery because Tomo's father tended to mourn from afar with a bottle at his lips, and Tomo's mother had never learned how to drive. Also, with the way Tomo's father spent money on alcohol, the family rarely had bus money.

Tomo shuffled the ball between his feet. "Well, even if it is the Day of the Dead..." His face was all screwed-up like he was thinking really hard. "Your dad was a really good football player, wasn't he?"

Marko enjoyed bragging about how amazing Tata had been at football. He pulled his shoulders back and stuck out his chest. "Yes. And?"

"And…" Tomo scratched his nose. "Wouldn't he want you to play, you know, in memory of him?"

Staring at the white and black shapes on the ball, Marko wondered whether that would be respectful. He had always thought that a person needed to be solemn or cry like Mama and Baka. But men should not cry and sit around all day with red eyes, blowing their noses into white handkerchiefs. He did not have any men around to watch how they mourned, and he certainly did not want to stare his eyes blind like that man at the cemetery. So how was he supposed to mourn?

Now, playing football was fun. Was it wrong, sacrilegious, pagan to have fun while mourning—something a *heathen* would do? He was not sure. But he could not imagine Tata sitting around, sulking the day down till dusk. Standing up, Marko grabbed the ball from Tomo's feet and tossed it up in the air. Catching it, he began to walk alongside Tomo. Up the road, the two kicked the ball back and forth until they reached the school football court. He would make Tata proud.

~~~

1997: Beth

Another plane had flown over, and Beth pressed her ear to the phone in an attempt to catch a word or two. Whenever a plane passed over, it both felt and sounded as if it were right above the house. "Sorry, Mom, another one went by, so I missed what you just said."

The voice came through a notch louder. "I was just asking about how Bruce is doing."

Beth listened for a moment to see if the plane had woken up the baby, but she didn't hear any crying. "He's doing fine. I think he's so used to living by the airport that he sleeps right through all the noise." She remembered a sound Maggie had had to sleep through: machine guns. Living in Split during the war, they had been protected by the mountains against the fighting. But for some reason, Croatians would fire off machine guns in the air for weddings, New Years, and other celebrations. One time she had been at the beach with Maggie and Zrinka. While they were talking, she suddenly heard the rapid sequence of automatic guns. She grabbed Maggie and flattened them both against the pebbled ground. Her heart pummeled inside her until she heard a few people laughing. Raising her head slightly, she saw people looking at her with grins and raised eyebrows. She peered to her left at Zrinka. Her friend explained to her that people would fire bullets into the air for celebration. Beth still could not comprehend why they would want to use weapons that meant death as a method of celebrating life. And besides, if you shot something into the air, did it not have to come down at some point? And yet, all around her, she saw babies sleeping in their strollers or in their mothers' arms as if the gunshots were lullabies.

Her mother wheezed into the phone. Asthma. She had been battling it over the past few years. Beth tried not to say anything since her mom did not like any fuss.

Her mom cleared her throat. "I just mailed you a package that has some little outfits for him."

Twirling the phone cord around her index finger, Beth glanced over at the laundry basket full of Bruce and Maggie's clothes. "Thanks, Mom. That boy—I tell you what—he's growing so fast, much faster than Maggie did at his age. He's developing quite the belly. Yesterday I could barely button up his pants. They are starting to have larger selections of baby clothes here, but they're still pretty expensive."

Her mom chuckled. "Well, that's where Old Navy comes in handy."

Beth picked at the edge of her T-shirt. "Ah, I miss Old Navy."

"When are you thinking to come back for a bit?"

Shifting in her seat gave Beth a better chance at seeing the calendar by the fridge. "I think Drew said we would go back not this Christmas but the next."

There was a pause. "I wish I could come see you again."

Beth brushed some crumbs off the kitchen table. "I wish you could too, Mom." Her mom had come to Croatia a year ago, when Beth was giving birth to Bruce. They had been scheduled to go back to the States so she could have him there, but he had come early. As soon as Drew told her mom that she was in labor, the determined fifty-five year old woman had booked the first ticket she could find from Michigan to Croatia. When she arrived, Beth had already given birth, but her mom was a huge blessing in that she helped take care of Bruce and Beth during that following month.

The delivery had drained Beth physically and emotionally. They had decided to go to the hospital in Split, which, although the second largest city in Croatia, still had many issues in the medical system. Drew had not been allowed to be with her throughout the entire delivery; in fact, she had often been left alone in the room with three other pregnant women. The nurses had given her nothing for the pain. "It'll pass," they would say, and she had screamed until her throat gave out. Her mom's arrival a few days later had helped Beth's recovery. Drew would sometimes take care of Maggie and Bruce so that Beth and her mom could spend time alone. Beth would end up laying her head on her mother's lap as her mom stroked her hair and listened, never saying all the things Beth was sure her mom wanted to say. Things like "Why are you staying here?" or "Why did you ever come here?" or "I told you so."

If only her mom could come visit again. But a few months ago, her mom had tripped while walking to the neighborhood pool and had sprained her ankle. Two weeks later, when she thought that it had healed, it gave out, causing her to slip in the shower and fall down hard on her hip. Now three months after surgery on both her hip and ankle, she still had a terrible limp.

"Well, maybe this hip will heal soon, and I'll be able to visit my girl."

Beth smiled and hoped. "That'd be wonderful." Crying from the kids' bedroom brought her upright. "Mom, Bruce is awake. I need to—"

"You go take care of my little grandson. Give him a kiss for me."

Standing up and walking toward the phone's cradle, Beth said softly, "I love you, Mama."

"Love you too, Elisabeth."

Hanging up the phone, Beth paused before going to the kids' room. For a moment, she wanted to pretend that she was a teenage girl. A teenage girl who did not have any responsibilities beyond completing her chores and her homework. A girl who only had to focus on communicating in one language. A girl whose problems could all be taken care of by her mother.

Soon Bruce's cries became too loud and sharp to ignore anymore. She opened the door to the room Bruce and Maggie shared. Standing up in his crib, Bruce reached to her with a wet, red face. She scooped him up into her arms and rubbed his small back for a while. Slowly his wailing calmed into a soft crying, and he nestled his head into the space between her head and shoulder. Her precious boy—one whose problems could all be taken care of by his mother.

~~~

1993: Tihomir

Tihomir pulled Zrinka in close to him. Only a weekend had passed, but he had missed her. She laughed lightly in his ear. "What?" he asked, his voice muffled in her thick black hair. He could imagine her smile.

"I missed you too."

He sniffed the air and pulled back a bit.

She laughed. "It's *pasticada.*"

He could feel his jaw drop. "Ohoho!" He picked her up and spun her around as she protested and laughingly demanded he put her down immediately. "My favorite. Haha *yupi!*" He set her down and dashed into the kitchen. Lifting the lid, he breathed in the beef he knew had been marinating for a whole day in red wine vinegar. He looked at the bottle next to the pot and breathed in the *prosek,* a sweet dessert wine that she must have just added to the meat.

As a child growing up, he had never had *pasticada* because it was a more of a southern, coastal dish. One night, after dating Zrinka for a while, she made him dinner: *pasticada.* As she served him the meat with the soft, white *njoki*, he had looked at her and known that he would one day marry her.

He turned around and gazed at his wife, who leaned against the doorway, her eyes laughing at him. From countless summers on the beach, she had acquired a deep tan that was emphasized by the white blouses she often wore. Her hair was long and curly, annoying her and enchanting him. She cooked delicious meals, took care of so many random details, made Tihomir feel as if everything was going to be all right, and spoke to everyone as if he or she was the only person in the world at that moment. If only…

He turned back toward the pot before she could see his face. But it was too late. She came to him and wrapped her arms around his waist from behind. "*Ljubavi*, what is it?"

He felt it lay down on his chest. Ah, how he wanted to kick it in the face. Of course. Of course it would show up now, now when he was alone with her, when they were about to eat his favorite meal and sip wine together. Its timing was always impeccable.

She laid her head on his back, pressing in gently against him, breathing in and out along with him. Tihomir listened to the slight drip from the faucet that made time with both his heart and hers. He loved being like this with her, one with her.

He heard a sniff. Oh *ne*. The one thing he couldn't stand was her crying. How could he comfort her when he himself needed to be comforted? He slowly wiggled out of her hold and, avoiding her gaze, muttered something about how he had forgotten to bring his bag in. As he left the kitchen, his feet felt heavy, each step away from her pulling him down toward the ground. He shut the door to the house. Outside by the car, the cool summer air filled his lungs and made him feel a bit more normal. Pulling out his duffel bag from the backseat, he slung it over his right shoulder and tilted his head toward the stars. Why, he wondered. Why, God?

VII

1997: Beth

Beth parked in front of the big cartoon elephant sign.

"Mom, what do elephants have to do with shoes?"

Shrugging her shoulders, Beth unbuckled her seatbelt and turned to the backseat where Maggie sat. "I don't know, Maggs. What do you think?"

Maggie tilted her head and squinted at the smiling elephant. She had that look on her face of concentration, as she often did when working on math problems. But then she shook her head and unbuckled her seatbelt. "I guess it doesn't matter." She got out of the car and shut the door.

Beth walked over to Maggie's side of the car and reached out to take one of her hands. Maggie squeezed Beth's hand tight and pulled herself in close to her mother's side. As the wind whipped about them both, Beth ushered Maggie quickly into the building.

Beth was excited for a day out with her daughter. She typically tried to hold off on most shopping until they had a few months in America, but Maggie needed some new shoes for school. She had pretty much outgrown the ones she was wearing. With Maggie's hand in hers, Beth looked down at her daughter's shoes. The cartoon Ariel was fading away, along with her little fish-friend, Flounder.

"Hey, kiddo, you want to watch *Little Mermaid* tonight?"

Maggie smacked her lips. "I have school tomorrow."

Such a responsible kid. Beth had been the exact opposite as a child. She had done everything she could to prove to her dad that she did not take orders from him. Like when he strictly told her not to get her ears pierced—she had flipped her hair back, shown him her decorated ears, and said, "Too late."

Beth swung their hands together back and forth. "Well, maybe you and I could stay up and watch it."

With big eyes, Maggie looked up.

"Tanja's taking care of Bruce. She could put him to bed, and we'll kick Daddy out. Just girls, you and me."

A big grin finally burst across Maggie's face. She inched closer to Beth and leaned her head against her as they walked down the first aisle of women's shoes.

Beth spotted a pair that might go nicely with the dress she had worn on her date with Drew. They were black, had a decent heel, and a subtle, little bow on the side. She reached over, checked the price on the box, and then continued down the aisle. She pointed to her right. "I think kids' shoes are this way."

Looking back, Maggie asked, "Don't you want to try them on? They're pretty."

"No, Maggs. We're here to buy *you* shoes."

"OK."

Beth guided Maggie toward the back corner on the left. She pointed out one of the first pairs she saw. "What about these? Do you like these?" The shoe were white with pink stars.

Shaking her head, Maggie kept going down the aisle. "No, I don't like pink anymore."

"So what's your favorite color now?"

"Gold."

Beth tried to picture what kind of shoes Maggie might want to buy.

They continued down to the end of the first aisle, Beth suggesting shoes and Maggie turning them down. They began down the other side, and Maggie exclaimed. "Those ones, Mommy!" She rushed toward the single shoe placed atop many boxes. It was a light purple with blue waves. Scanning the size numbers on the boxes, Beth thanked God the shoes weren't gold. She found the right box and pulled it out. Just as she began to pull out the tissue paper, she heard a voice behind her.

Beth turned around to a lady with a lot of make-up and a severe frown. From her white and blue clothes, she could tell the woman worked at Pitarelo. Beth asked what the problem was, and the woman began to rant and wave her arms about. Look what they had done to her neat stack of shoes. They had made a mess of things, they were blocking the aisle from other customers, and they probably weren't even going to buy the shoes. Beth looked down at Maggie, who wore the same confused look she did. Why was this woman giving them such a hard time? They only wanted to buy a pair of shoes. Beth said something about how they would clean up the mess when they were done trying the shoes on. The woman tossed her big blonde hair to her right and continued with her tirade: everybody wanted to make her job harder, as if she didn't have enough trouble what with taking care of her four children, her husband, her mother-in-law, and feeding them all too!

Maggie tugged on Beth's pants and said amidst the woman's yelling, "Mom, let's look at another pair."

"Just hang in there, Maggs." She turned to the woman and assured her that they would put everything back in its place.

The woman's eyebrows rose. "Ah, you are American. I know to speak English."

Beth tried to keep the conversation going in Croatian, but the woman kept responding in English. "No, no, my English is better than your Croatian. This makes sense why you don't understand what I say."

Beth clutched the tissue paper that she still had in her hand.

The woman daintily brushed a curl off her face. "I am try to say you that you make mess of my shoes and paper."

Beth rolled back her shoulders. "Yes, I understand you perfectly. What *I* am trying to say is that we want to buy shoes, so I need you to let my daughter try them on, so she can see if they fit, so we can buy them or buy some others shoes. OK?"

The woman took a step back. "*Okej, okej.* It is not big problem. Try shoes on. Don't make big mess, *okej?*"

Beth gritted her teeth. "Yes, yes, we won't make a big mess." As the woman walked away, Beth crouched down to help Maggie put the shoes on. "Sorry about that, Maggs."

Looking down, Maggie bit her lip. "I don't want to try these shoes anymore."

"Nonsense. C'mon, give me your right foot."

Maggie scooted her legs in closer to her body. "No, I want to go home."

"Maggie, don't be ridiculous. Give me your foot."

Not looking at Beth's face, Maggie wrapped her arms around her legs.

Beth threw the shoe down on the floor. "We came here because you need new shoes. I don't even want to spend money, but you've outgrown your old ones, so what can I do? I have to deal with that crazy lady who thinks I can't speak Croatian, and I don't need this from you. So try the dang shoe on!"

Laying her head down on her arms, Maggie went silent.

Beth stood up and walked down to the small bench at the end of the aisle. She sat down, closed her eyes, and pressed her fingers against her eyelids. As a kid, she had always pressed against her eyes until she began to see psychedelic colors spin around. When she had boasted about it, her mom had scolded her and told her that she would make herself go blind. Beth had been terrified and never done it since. Now she didn't care and watched the colors spin.

Would this have happened in Target? Beth pictured walking down the kids' shoe aisle with Maggie. A lady with a red shirt would come up with a smiled-filled face and ask them if they needed any help. Maggie would have endless choices, cheap choices. No, this would not have happened in Target.

Was she a bad mother, bringing her child to a war-torn country, and not giving her what she deserved? Opening her eyes, Beth glanced back at her firstborn. Maggie's hair hung down, covering her face. A couple years ago, they had tried bangs on Maggie, but the look had not suited her. Now the bangs had grown out, and her hair was getting longer every day, creating new curls at the ends. Most everyone at church had called her a *princesa*, especially when she wore the frilly, poofy little dresses Beth's mom frequently sent. At the moment, Maggie was rubbing her hazel eyes. Beth had never seen eyes change colors so often. Depending on what Maggie wore, her eyes could be blue, green, or a striking golden. Now they were red, the color of Beth's failure.

Rubbing the palms of her hands against her thighs, Beth straightened up her back. She might not have been able to give Maggie the perfect life, but she could restrain her temper and love her daughter when life was hard and frustrating. She stood up and walked back over to her little girl. Softly she said, "I'm sorry, Maggs." When she heard no response, she crouched down next to Maggie. "I didn't act the way I should. I let things get to me when I shouldn't have." She smoothed Maggie's curls back off her small forehead. "Will you forgive me?"

Maggie peeked up over her crossed. She nodded lightly.

Pulling her into a hug, Beth squeezed her tight against her and whispered to her, "I love you, Maggsy." She heard Maggie respond with a faint, "I love you, too." When she pulled back, she looked at her daughter's face and wiped away some of the tears. Then she picked up the pair of shoes. "Do you want to try these on?"

Maggie studied the pair for a moment and then nodded. She slid her right foot into one of them and wiggled her toes around. Beth pinched the end of the shoe to see where Maggie's toes were. Maggie let out a soft giggle and then tied the laces before trying on the second shoe. Once she had them both on, she walked down the aisle, looked in the mirror at the end, and came back to Beth.

They seemed to be a good fit. Beth asked her, "What do you think?"

Maggie's dimples appeared, and Beth began to hope. Maybe she could do this. Maybe she could buy her daughter shoes. Maybe she could love without getting mad all the time. She helped Maggie get her old shoes back on and packed up the new shoes in the box. Ignoring the obnoxiously blonde Pitarelo woman, she paid for the shoes and walked hand-in-hand with Maggie. "Let's go watch *Little Mermaid*." The wind outside couldn't blow their grins away.

~~~

1993: Tihomir

"*Catedral Sveti Duje*." Tihomir stared up at the Romanesque wooden doors. They portrayed fourteen scenes from the life of Christ and were separated by rich ornaments. "The Cathedral of Saint Domnius."

Today Tihomir had decided to take Drew on a tour of downtown Split. They had walked through the *pazar*, gently ignoring the shouts of old men and women selling everything from tomatoes to hats of all shapes and sizes. Then they had stopped for some coffee on the boardwalk like they had done on the first day of Drew's visit. This time, a week into Drew's stay, Tihomir wanted to show him the heart of the city: the cathedral. Here was the city's pulse, its history, and its present pursuit of God. As they walked into the gothic structure, Tihomir spoke in a low voice to Drew, "Every Sunday the people pack themselves into churches such as these, not so much looking for truth." He brushed his hand over one of the Gospel scenes. "No, coming to mass is their duty. To be Croatian is to be Catholic."

As they walked through the cathedral, Tihomir quietly explained its history to Drew. In the third century, Emperor Diocletian was one of the worst persecutors of Christians. He beheaded many, including Saint Domnius, the Bishop of Salona. Tihomir explained that this cathedral was once the mausoleum of Diocletian, where his relics remained.

Ironically, it later became a church, Saint Domnius's bones were brought in, and he became the patron saint of the city.

Tihomir spoke softly, "So, you see, something that was once evil was restored to good." He gazed up at the tall, intricate architecture. "Redemption is possible."

When they headed back outside, they met the old man who sold tickets up to the bell tower. Tihomir handed him ten kunas for the both of them and then lead Drew up the long, narrow staircase. The stairs were deep, and each one took an effort to reach up to, causing the men to soon find themselves out of breath. The walls were dark and cold, winding counterclockwise about them. After several minutes of climbing, they reached the more open part, where the stairs became metal and the bells towered above them.

Looking up, Tihomir recalled one summer, when he was four or five years old, and Mama had brought him and a couple other siblings down to Split. She took them up the bell tower, her eyes infatuated by the big, beautiful bells. Unfortunately, not even Mama had realized that it was almost eleven in the morning when they had begun to climb up the stairs. She and the children were hiking up when suddenly the bells rang out, causing the little ones to quickly slap their hands against their ears. They each looked to Mama with scrunched up faces, but she was laughing. Grabbing hold of Tihomir's hand, she had taken one of his hands off of his ear. He looked up at her, bewildered. She just grinned and yelled, "*Dragi*, never forget this."

And Tihomir had not forgotten.

When Tihomir and Drew reached the top, they looked out over all of Split. Around them, the scenery was spotted with red tile rooftops that topped off the stone wall homes, and outside the windows on long wire clotheslines hung wet shirts, pants, skirts… In front of them, the sun radiated onto the sea, causing it to shimmer with the promise of an engagement ring, and large ferryboats slowly made their way off to the islands. Behind them, mountains rose and dropped along the horizon, dotted with green and blue.

Drew rested his elbows on the wall that separated him from a long fall. He murmured, "Wow. You can see it all."

Tihomir nodded. The panoramic view was exquisite, perfect. He pointed to their right. "You see that house over there?"

"Yes."

Tihomir spoke softly, aware of the other tourists around them who were taking pictures and enjoying the view. "The people in that house do not know that they can have a relationship with Christ."

Drew's gaze rested on the house.

Tihomir pointed to their left. "See that café?"

Drew nodded.

"The owners, waiters, waitresses, customers—they don't know that Jesus came so that they could be saved by faith, not by works." Tihomir pointed toward the sea. "Every day people sail their boats or go on a ferry to the island, and almost none of them know that Christ came so they might have life, rich and full life." He was waving his hands about, his voice rising. "They live in negativity, not believing in anything. They wander these streets with heads down, unaware." He turned to Drew with a strong look. "I need to know. I need to know if you care enough to stay."

Drew stared out at the sea, his eyes fixed, intent, and thoughtful.

Tihomir remained silent, also watching the sea. The wind was rustling it and causing it to sway and bend. Taking hold of some strands of his hair, the wind pulled at him. He offered it his plea, hoping that it would carry his request to God's ears. Even if God did not answer his personal prayers, surely he would answer his prayers for the Croatian people.

They stood that way for a long while. Tourists came and went from the top of the bell tower, taking pictures, commenting on the beauty, and then beginning their descent. That was all they saw. The beauty. They were inattentive to the vast pain of the city's people. They took pictures and left, thinking that they had "seen" Split, tasted of it. They would have their cup of coffee, purchase a few postcards and leave.

Drew turned to Tihomir.

As the wind swooped around Drew's face, a smile spread, showing the white teeth of the American.

God had answered.

~~~

2000: Marko

Marko sat down at the table, waiting for Mama to put the food on the table. He was ready to fill his stomach. At school that day, Teacher had yelled at him for getting a 2 on his test. She had pointed to Anamarija who had gotten a 5. Teacher had called him stupid and some other things Marko couldn't remember. After a few seconds of her loud voice, he had stared at his shoes and thought about playing football after school. To score the first goal of the game was the greatest sign of victory, or was it to score the last? He remembered when Croatia played in the World Cup in 1998 and Davor Suker scored the winning goal that made all the men in the neighborhood leap from their chairs, spill their beer, and hug and kiss each other. Marko and his buddies had been watching the game at the café on the corner. They had been peering on tiptoe around the television screen when suddenly all the men that blocked their view stood up and began to go insane. *Hrvatska!* Marko had puffed out his chest and screamed as loud as he could with his friends, declaring that Croatia was the best, the best in the whole world.

Marko scooted his chair close to the table. "Mama?"

His mom turned from the stove. "What?"

Picking up a little crumb, Marko flicked it off the table. "Tata could have been a great football player, yes?"

"Ah, what do I know?" She turned back to the stove, shrugging her shoulders. "He was good on the court. Often scored goals or assisted others."

Marko could not see her face, but he knew she was smiling.

"He loved to show off. He would often look up to the crowd to see if I was watching. Then, when he'd spotted me, he would throw himself completely into the game. And he never watched any football games." She shook her head. "No, he *had* to be playing. There was no watching for him." She stirred the soup slowly. "He played in a club for a few years. But then he hurt his knee, and he got the job working at a bank. When his leg had healed, it was too late to start up again." She pulled out a few bowls from the cupboard and set them down next to the stove. Then she just stood there, staring out the window. Her eyes seemed to be looking for something, longing for something. "Yes. Yes, he could have been great."

She took a handkerchief out of her pocket and wiped her eyes. She always carried a handkerchief with her because, as she often told him, her tears were connected to every emotion inside her: sadness, anger, happiness, excitement… Placing the handkerchief back in her pocket, she turned to the stove and began scooping spoons of the tomato soup into the bowls. She told Marko to go get Baka. Standing up from the table, he shuffled down the hallway to Baka's dark room. He opened the door and peered into the darkness. Ever since he could remember, she had always had the shutters closed and did not like any lights on. "Baka?"

He heard a grunt come from the bed. He went over and poked the blanket. She swore at him, telling him not to poke an old woman. Slowly, she sat up and he could feel her looking at him in the dark. "Petar?"

"No, Baka, it's Marko."

"Where's Petar?"

For some reason, when she woke up from naps, Baka would always ask about Marko's dad. Sleeping seemed to confuse her, and Mama had told him not to make a big fuss out of it but instead to just make something up. "He is out in the garden."

Baka grunted again and tried to lift herself from the bed. Muttering and swearing, she leaned on Marko as she stood up and began to shuffle toward the kitchen. She patted his head and said, "Good Petar. Good son."

When the two entered the kitchen, Mama had everything on the table: tomato soup, French salad, meat, potatoes, and, of course, bread. She had sliced the dark bread up and put the slices in a bowl. Marko grabbed one and began to stuff it into his mouth while Mama scowled at him. He grinned and he could tell she wanted to grin back by the way her skin was tightening up around her cheeks. Mama didn't laugh much, but when she did, ah, life was good.

After they crossed themselves and muttered a typical thank you to God, Mary, and Mama and Baka's favorite saints, Marko grabbed more bread, dipped it in the soup, and enjoyed.

Mama tore a chunk of bread and popped it into her mouth. "You know Tihomir Milic from down the street?"

Baka squawked, "What you say?"

Mama spoke louder, "You know that Tihomir and his wife from down the street?"

"*Ajme*, Katarina, don't yell. My ears are fragile."

Mama rolled her eyes. "Yes, *okej*, Mama, do you know him?"

"Who?"

"Tihomir Milic."

"Ah yes, yes." She grunted. "That heathen of a man."

Marko looked up. *Gospodin* Milic was also a heathen?

Mama popped a piece of salad into her mouth. "Yes, his little cult seems to grow bigger every day. It's disgusting. He calls himself a Croatian. How, I ask you?"

"Maybe he's become American. Doesn't he hang out with those Americans?"

"No, no, that was years ago." Mama laughed and slapped the table. "It is the funniest thing. He used to live right next to the American family and they were all best of friends, I guess, but now the two men hardly speak. I've heard the wives are not allowed to meet. Ha. You see? If they would just go to confession, they wouldn't have this problem."

Baka nodded and pushed her food around. "Exactly."

"And..." Mama licked her lips. "I bet his wife Zrinka picked up some of those bad American habits, you know, like sitting on something cold or walking barefoot. Yes, I bet that's why she can't have children."

Baka's thin eyebrows pushed in together. "She can't have children?"

"You know this. The woman has been pregnant a few times. I've seen her develop a small belly. But, ah..." Mama looked down at her plate and shook her head. "It is a shame." She then looked up at Marko. "I only had you, but you are a good one." Reaching over, she pinched his cheeks before he could pull away. She and Baka laughed at him. Then they began a discussion on how the priest had gotten pneumonia and now they had a temporary old priest whom no one could understand.

Stuffing more into his mouth, Marko thought about how we wanted a dog or even to play with someone else's dog, like *Gospodin* Tihomir's Dalmatian. But was the dog a heathen too?

VIII

1993: Tihomir

The flight from Munich had landed, and Tihomir looked over the heads of the people around him. Exclamations vibrated throughout the tall-ceilinged room as mothers reunited with children and husbands rushed to their wives with big grins. Everyone was kissing everyone on both cheeks, shaking hands, and commenting on each other's clothing or weight. Tihomir remembered how Drew had been shocked by how blunt Croatians could be. He would have to get used to it now that he was coming to live in Croatia.

Zrinka squeezed Tihomir's hand. She was leaning into him and now looked up to him with a smile. Tihomir saw the excitement in her eyes that mirrored his own. After months of waiting, praying, and hoping, this day had at last come to them. They were both eager for these new partners in ministry, these friends… He squeezed her hand back and then kept scanning the crowd.

After a few minutes, he spotted his friend. "Drew!" He waved and motioned to the American. Drew spotted him, grinned, and whispered something to the woman next to him.

Throughout Drew's time in Croatia ten months ago, the American would often take out his wallet, smile like a little boy, and pull out a picture of his wife, Beth. Then he would tell Tihomir a story about her, sometimes recent, sometimes from back when the two were first beginning to fall in love. Drew had said she was the most beautiful woman on earth. Tihomir glanced down at his own wife. He had always been biased when it came to women—Zrinka had a certain grace, a quiet beauty that struck him deeply even now, years after his first meeting her.

Still, he had to admit that Beth was lovely. She was not beautiful in a supermodel way but in a natural, go-with-it-as-it-comes way. He looked at her now: her sweats and sweatshirt spoke of comfort and her curly dark brown hair surrounded her head in free simplicity. Drew had told Tihomir the first reason he fell in love with Beth had been her hair. It was long, and Drew loved long hair. The second reason had been her smile. At the moment, she was smiling at every single person she bumped into, regardless of their response to her.

Now she looked up, scanned the crowd, and waved energetically when she spotted Tihomir and Zrinka. She bent down to speak to someone Tihomir could not see through the crowd. Tihomir imagined she was speaking to Maggie, their three-year-old child.

The family took a long time to reach Tihomir and Zrinka. The Americans did not push and shove as most of the Croatians surrounding them were doing. They just kept smiling and apologizing their way through until they finally came to Tihomir and Zrinka with all their bags—Tihomir counted at least six. He could not imagine what all they had packed in those bags. Shaking Drew's hand, he clapped him on the back, and kissed him on both cheeks. "My friend, you have gotten skinny, far too skinny." Looking over at Zrinka, he motioned to her. "We must fix this!"

Drew laughed and shook Zrinka's hand, kissing her on both cheeks.

Zrinka grinned up at the American. "Good to see you again, Drew."

Drew nodded. "Good to be back." Motioning toward his wife, Drew introduced her. "Tihomir and Zrinka, this is Beth, my beautiful, wonderful wife." He looked down upon her with pride and admiration. Beth blushed and shook Zrinka's hand, awkwardly attempting the kissing on both cheeks. "Oh I'm sorry. Did I do that right?"

Zrinka laughed lightly and shook her head. "No worry, Beth. You teach me better English, and I will teach you to say 'Hi.'"

Tihomir saw in Beth what he often saw when people met Zrinka: relaxed shoulders and eyes that said, I have found a friend.

Drew picked up their little girl, tickling her. She let out a squeal. "And this is our little girl, Maggie."

Maggie hid in her dad's arms but peeked out at Zrinka. Tihomir watched his wife approach the child and touch her gently on the arm. She whispered something, and the child reached out and fingered Zrinka's gold cross necklace. Zrinka spoke to her softly, and soon Maggie was stretching out her arms for Zrinka to hold her. After looking to Beth for consent, Zrinka took the little one into her arms and spoke softly to her. Tihomir had seen this many times, but for some reason he knew that Maggie would hold a special place in Zrinka's heart.

"Okej people, are you hungry?"

Drew and Beth both nodded. Though their eyes spoke of exhaustion, Tihomir could also see in them an eagerness and an excitement.

Tihomir grabbed one of the suitcases from Beth. "Zrinka made you a feast that will make you feel at home right away. So you come to our house first, then we will help you move into your new place."

Beth repositioned a backpack that hung from one shoulder and a huge purse that hung from another. She looked up at Tihomir. "Did you find us an apartment?"

Tihomir couldn't hide his grin. "Yes, I found you the best: an apartment right next to ours!"

"Oh, that's wonderful." Beth placed her hand on her husband's shoulder. "It's good to know we have somewhere to settle into." She looked at Zrinka who was speaking to little Maggie. "And neighbors. We already have wonderful neighbors."

Drew slapped Tihomir on the back. "Thank you, friend. You have done so much for us."

Tihomir slapped him back and nodded toward the glass doors. He led the family out toward the car and felt the hope build up inside him.

~~~

Tihomir led the American family up the stairs in the old building. He had patiently waited two whole days since they arrived, and now he would at last reveal to them this meeting place for believers. Two months ago, he had begun renting it for Sunday mornings and Wednesday nights. Only a couple dozen people were coming so far, but he believed that with time, they would soon outgrow the place.

Already, after such a short time, he no longer noticed the urine smell in the stairwell. He did, however, note that Beth's eyes had widened at the sight of a used syringe lying on one of the steps. He quickly explained, "Drug addicts usually come here to shoot up or get out of the weather when it's raining. Sometimes they sleep in here." Beth looked up at him and then at Drew and then at little Maggie. She drew the toddler up into her arms and remained quiet. Kicking the needle off the step, Tihomir continued, "But no worries, Beth. They are usually gone when we arrive in the morning on Sundays and don't come until long after we're gone on Wednesdays."

He reached the top of the stairs and turned around. "And just think! If they are here and they see us and hear our singing and preaching of the word, imagine how their lives could change." With that, he unlocked the door and pushed it open. "It is not a beautiful cathedral, but I believe God meets us here." His fingers searched for the switch, and then boom, light filled the big room. Waving back, he motioned Drew and his family to come in. Beth gazed about, and Tihomir could not read her reaction. Looking toward the back of the room reminded him that he had not yet replaced the curtains. They were a dull green that reminded him of vomit, and holes were scattered throughout them like Swiss cheese.

Zrinka came up to Beth and said, "You want go with me to store and buy new... zavjesa..."

"Curtains," Tihomir offered.

"Yes, curtains. You want?"

Beth nodded with a smile, and Tihomir watched as the two women strolled around the room together, pointing out to each other changes that needed to be made.

He walked over toward Drew, who was carrying Maggie in his arms. Tihomir waved at the little one. She was wearing a yellow dress with sleeves that puffed out. On her head lay a white bow among little brown curls. He had already started calling her princesa for she always looked like one with the dresses she wore and the way she danced about. And those eyes: there was a depth there, as if she knew something he did not. Tihomir asked Drew, "What do you think?"

Drew shifted Maggie in his arms, looking about the room. "It's great that we have a place to meet in now instead of preaching on the streets."

"We need to make many changes."

"The good thing is that a church is not about the place. It's about the people, the body of Christ, and Christ himself all coming and meeting together." He turned toward Tihomir. "Here we can meet together with Christ."

Tihomir slapped him on the back. "Amen, my friend."

They walked about the room as Tihomir explained how multiple groups of people rented out the floor. The other renters consisted of various religious groups and political associations. But on Sundays and Wednesdays the space belonged to Tihomir and the church. The space consisted of the large room, a bathroom, and a small room they used for Sunday school and storage. Zrinka had started the Sunday school as soon as they had started meeting there. She taught the children stories from the Bible and short songs that would help them remember important concepts. In the past few months Tihomir had heard many mothers and fathers talk about how pleased they were with his Zrinka.

He brought Drew up to the front of the room. "We have around thirty people coming every Sunday, sometimes a little more, sometimes a little less."

Drew gazed out at the now empty room. "That's a good start."

"We will see it grow soon," Tihomir said confidently. He rubbed his hands together. "Now, we must set the chairs up. You help me?"

"Of course."

Tihomir led Drew to the smaller room and began to carry folding chairs back to the large room. While the two men set up, Zrinka was showing Beth the materials for Sunday school. Meanwhile, Maggie sat on the floor, playing with some of the toys Zrinka had pulled out for her. With two chairs in each arm, Drew said, "I think Beth is really excited about helping Zrinka."

"Zrinka is happy for the help." Tihomir unfolded the chairs and began a straight row down the front. "The people are still, how you say, unsure about what they should do to serve in the church."

Drew struggled for a moment with a chair that was stuck. Finally he was able to push it open. "You and Zrinka do most of the work."

"*Da*. But I think they will soon see that church is not about just coming and listening."

Following Tihomir back to the room, Drew commented, "The body is a family. We have to work together."

"Exactly."

After they set up the chairs, they brought out a music stand that Tihomir would use to hold his Bible and notes.

"What are you going to preach on this morning?"

Tihomir took his notes out of his pocket and placed them on the stand. "I will introduce you and your family. You can come up and say some things about how you come here. I will translate for you."

"Sounds good."

"And then I will read the verses in Matthew 6, when Jesus teaches his disciples how to pray." He got out his Bible and placed the red ribbon on the page where the passage was so he wouldn't have to spend time flipping to it during the service. "I want to talk about praying for God's kingdom to come and how you came as an answer to my prayer for exactly that."

Drew walked to the back of the room toward the windows, and Tihomir followed. Peering out the second-story windows, Drew looked down at the people who passed by. "For the past several months I kept thinking about the view from the bell tower and the things you said." He opened the window and let the sounds of the city fill the room. "I am glad to be here."

Tihomir heard voices and turned to see Ivo and Sladana, an older couple of the church, come in. He went to greet them, shaking their hands and kissing them on both cheeks. When they saw Drew, they exclaimed and rushed him with loud voices and kissing, telling him how glad they were that he was back. Tihomir didn't know how much Drew could understand, but he could tell by his wide grin that the American was overjoyed by the couple's love. Tihomir watched the interaction, looked around the room, and could see God's kingdom coming.

~~~

1997: Beth

"Thank you so much for helping her," Beth said to the woman who sat at the end of the table. Tanja replied with the typical "no problem" and continued to sip at her coffee. Beth dried off the last plate and placed it in the cupboard. Ugly orange cupboards. Glaring at them, Beth tried to will away the color. They just stared back at her with utter defiance. She turned back toward the table. "Maggie has been needing help in history, haven't you, sweets?"

Nodding, Maggie closed her notebook and textbook. "Thank you, Teta Tanja."

Tanja offered Maggie a big grin. "No problem, Megica. You are very smart, and I am impressed with how quickly you learn in another language." She turned in her chair to face Beth. "I don't think most children could do what she's doing. She has almost all 5's in her classes, yes?"

Beth stood up a little straighter and brought her shoulders back a little. "Yes, Maggie is quite the student. We're very proud of her."

Maggie allowed a shy smile, picked up her books, and walked toward the hallway. Then she retraced her steps. "Oh, Mom, can Petra come over?"

"Yes, that'd be fine."

The smile spread across her face. "OK, I'll go call her." She bounded back toward the hallway, where the phone was. The two women could soon hear her talking away in Croatian.

Beth noticed that Tanja's cup was almost empty. Motioning toward it she asked, "Would you like another cup of coffee?"

Handing her cup over, Tanja replied, "Oh yes, thank you." She leaned back in her chair. "Maggie seems quite fond of Petra. She told me that she

As she tipped the coffee pot, Beth said, "Yes, Petra is her best friend. Maggie seems to get along great with most of the girls in her class, but Petra comes over the most." Beth handed Tanja her coffee. "I wonder if it's because Petra can relate a bit to Maggie."

Tanja took a sip and tilted her head. "How does she relate to her?"

Filling her own cup, Beth sat down next to Tanja. "Well, I've heard that Petra's mom is an atheist."

"Oho, not a good thing to be here."

Beth warmed her hands on the cup. "I know. Her husband goes to mass every Sunday with their kids, but I think she only goes for Christmas and Easter."

"Hmm... So how does that make her similar to Maggie?"

Beth looked out the window into the garden. She looked forward to seeing the flowers again, especially the pink geraniums, and the purple ones too. Tucking herself tighter into her cashmere sweater, she prayed for spring to come upon them quickly. "Maggie and Petra are both 'different' from everybody else. Neither of them goes to mass nor attends catechism in school. The neighbors don't know what to make of it. They've grown up in homes without some of the traditions most kids have. I mean..." She brushed a crumb off the table. "... they both get along fine with the other children. It's just that they're both a little... 'different.' "

Tanja nodded and took another sip. "Hmm... we should probably get to our lesson soon, but how are you doing? You know, with everything that has happened?"

Beth breathed in the rich scent of the coffee. "I'm OK. I think the lessons will help. I want to be able to speak better."

"Mm yes, we should switch to Croatian now." Tanja's voice deepened as she began to speak in her native language. "Have you decided what to do for church?"

Beth didn't know how to form the answer in English, let alone in Croatian. "Drew decide to... He says he to want to make new church, to start new."

"He wants to start a new church," Tanja gently corrected her, nodding for her to continue.

Beth played with the frayed fabric of the tablecloth. "Yes, he says we to go slow and to see what happen, uh, we look God to tell us how."

"You look to God to tell you what to do next. Yes. Hmm…" Tanja pushed some of her dark brown curls out of her face. "Beth, I am so sorry." She traced the rim of her cup with her index finger. "This situation is so bad. I do not know what all happened, and I do not want to know." She lifted the cup to her mouth but stopped and set it back down. She looked up at Beth with wet eyes. "We miss you."

Beth swallowed and blinked. "We also miss you, too. This… this is not our want." She extended her hand, and Tanja squeezed it hard. They sat quietly for a few moments, listening to the drip of the faucet. It would drip all day and all night long, no matter what Drew tried to do. The landlord kept saying he would fix it "tomorrow."

Tanja wiped her face with her fingertips. "I have been thinking." She bit her lip and looked up at Beth. "I have been thinking about leaving the church, too."

Beth's eyes went wide and switched to English. "No, no, no, Tanja. That's not what we wanted at all. Please, please…"

Tanja waved her hands to stop Beth's words. "I know you and Drew do not mean for this to happen, and I do not do it because of you. You leaving helped me in my decision, but I have been wondering for a long time if God would support a man who does not preach truth anymore."

"Oh, Tanja. That is a very strong claim against Tihomir."

"You do not think he is saying some things he should not?"

Beth licked her lips that suddenly seemed dry. "Please, Tanja, could we talk about something else?"

Tanja sat back in her chair. She sat there for a moment, looking at Beth, her eyes intent. Then she asked softly, "Have you talked to Zrinka lately?"

Beth stared into her coffee cup and tried to find her breath. "Not as much as I'd like."

"Does he forbid it?"

Beth interlocked her fingers and held them tightly in her lap. "Tanja. I… I really would like to get to our lesson."

Sighing, Tanja placed her hand on Beth's arm. "Forgive me. I push too much. Everything seems so wrong, and I just…" She looked at Beth and then sighed again. She turned to open her notebook. "Okej, let's start with where we left off last week." She pushed the curls once again out of her face. "The genetiv case. Do you remember it?"

Reaching across the table, Beth grabbed her own notebook. "Is that the one that shows possession?"

Tanja leaned forward and nodded. "Yes, yes, that is right. And do you remember how it affects the endings of nouns and adjectives?"

Over the next couple of hours, the women discussed grammar, got off subject, and laughed deeply. The coffee pot was drained and their spirits filled.

~~~

2000: Marko

Running into the hallway, Marko was met by the sound of scolding from Mama.

"Ma, Marko, really. You are not still on your football court. Slow down, take off your shoes, and put your slippers on."

He did as she said, mumbling under his breath about how slippers were for small children and old women. Baka had made them years ago, and they were scratchy and hot and made his feet sweat.

Walking into the kitchen, he tried to grab some bread, but Mama smacked his hand away and shook her finger in his face. Scolding him, she waved her hands in front of her as a sign for him to get out of her kitchen. As she turned back to the stove, she sent a lid crashing to the floor and swore, cursing the lid, the pan, and her clumsy self. Backing out of the kitchen, Marko got a brief glance at her eyes and saw that they were as red as the strawberries in the garden. He remembered the last time she had acted like this.

Quietly, he walked down the hallway and knocked on the door to Baka's room. When no answer came, he slowly opened the door and waited for his eyes to adjust to the darkness. He heard wheezing coming from the bed. "Baka?"

A sharp cough met him. He began to see the wrinkled face that was buried in the black clothing and the white pillow. "Baka, are you *okej*?"

She muttered something, but he couldn't make it out, so he pressed his ear close to her mouth. She was saying something about her rosary.

He stood up and felt his way around the room to the desk that sat in the corner. Above it hung the beaded necklace. Picking it up, he smoothed over the beads with his thumbs. Baka had once told him that this rosary had been her husband's. Marko did not remember his dida, for the old man had died when Marko was only a small child. He did have a picture in his mind of a bearded man swinging him around when he was little, and he had always wondered if that man could have been his dida. He returned to Baka's side and extended the rosary toward her.

She reached up and covered the rosary and his hands with her own. Her hands trembled, like a house shaken by a never-ending earthquake. She whispered, "Pray."

He did as she asked, trying to remember the wording of the prayer for the sick. He began to recite it, but her claw of a hand reached up and grasped his arm. "No, no." Touching one of the beads, she brought her lips up to kiss it. "Pray... for... salvation."

"Whose?"

She closed her eyes.

"Mine."

IX

1997: Beth

"Hello, Luka, please come in." Beth took the man's coat and offered him some slippers. Croatians thought that going barefoot led to at least a cold, if not death. Their first summer in Croatia a neighbor had brought over wool slippers for Maggie. The average temperature that summer had been in the upper nineties. Beth had Maggie wear the slippers whenever people came over. Then, as soon as the three of them had the house to themselves, they would all go happily barefoot. The cool tile floor was ever-soothing to their hot soles.

Beth had her own pair of slippers on now. She led Luka down the hallway and motioned for him to take a seat on the couch. "We are wait for Helena." Noticing a little white sock on the floor, she bent to pick it up.

Leaning back into the couch, Luka smiled. "Your Croatian improves every day."

Beth stood up and looked at his big smiling face. Luka had a large, bald head, ears that stuck out, and a smile that never left. He hardly ever showed his teeth, most likely because they were almost all black from years of dental neglect. She smiled back at him. "Thank you, Luka. This means much to me."

The front door burst open. "I am so sorry!"

Holding her hand up to her mouth, Beth tried to keep back her laughter. Helena was soaked. Her hair stuck to her face and dripped on the tile floor. She was carrying an umbrella that had been turned inside out, by the bura, no doubt. "Helena, what happen to you?"

Flinging down her umbrella, Helena walked into the living area, tracking wet footprints with her boots. "What happened to me? Oh, I will tell you what happened to me." She set one hand on her hip and waved the other to help illustrate her story. "I was going to pazar to buy some cabbage because my mother, she complain all day about not having enough cabbage to stay good and healthy and that if she does not eat some soon, she will die. So I say to myself, Helena, you must go buy some cabbage before Mama dies. So I go to pazar." She stopped to take a breath and then continued on at full-excited-Helena speed. "And at pazar I look around. I go from table to table, and…they have no cabbage!"

She looked at all of their faces, seemingly expecting a huge reaction. Beth offered a "no cabbage?"

Satisfied, Helena continued, "No cabbage! I say to myself, this is, no I say to the people selling vegetables, this is crazy! Where is all the cabbage? And they look at me like I'm stupid, and then they say something stupid about already selling all the cabbage. Ha!"

Luka leaned forward. "What did you do?"

Helena sat down on the couch, soaking wet. Beth tried not to grimace. Her friend tended to be a little unaware when she was caught up in the excitement of something.

After crossing her legs, Helena continued. "So I say to myself, Helena, you need to go to the grocery store to find cabbage."

"The grocery store?" Now Beth was genuinely shocked.

Helena held up her hand. "I know, I know. I always swear I will not buy food at grocery store. Bljak!" She made a disgusted face. "But today I was desperate. So I walk to the Konzum around the corner from the pazar and ha! You will not believe. It was closed."

Luka's eyes widened. "Why?"

Helena shook her head. "Because of all this rain, the store was flooded."

"Flooded?" Beth asked.

"Flooded." Helena let her hands fall into her lap. "And so I walk in the rain trying to find cabbage so Mama won't die, and I finally find a little store that has cabbage, and I buy it. But then!" Now she stood up again. "Then I got on the bus to come here, and the bus was so crowded because it was raining so hard, you know? So when I reach my stop here, I try to push my way out, and I drop the cabbage on the floor. It rolls under people's legs, and I try to get it, but bus driver, he yell at me, 'woman, I'm not wait forever for you to get off!'" Helena rolled her eyes. "Ajme. So I try to find it quickly, but he keep yelling at me, and so I give up and get off." She sighed. "So here I am, wet, very wet, and no cabbage, and Mama will die."

Luka's face spread out in a wide smile, and he looked at Beth, who was biting her lower lip. When their eyes met, they couldn't contain it, and laughter burst forth. Helena gave them a fierce look before collapsing back onto the couch in her own laughter.

Beth went over to her and patted her knee. "Oh Helena, you are funny. You want warm clothes to change?"

Helena nodded. "Yes, please."

While Helena changed into some of Beth's clothes, Beth made a pot of coffee. She asked Luka about his work. He was a waiter at one of the café bars down on the Riva. As he served people, he looked for opportunities to start conversations with them. People of all ages seemed to open up to him. Sometimes people would even invite for him to sit down and talk with them, so he would spend his breaks listening to their stories and sharing his own. As he spoke of his own life, he shared with them the Gospel.

He was telling her one such occurrence when Helena entered back into the room wearing Beth's sweats and a t-shirt. She was using a hand towel to sop up the rainwater from her hair. Looking around, she asked, "Where is little Bruce?"

Beth opened a cupboard and took down a few mugs. "I put him to bed. He didn't get a nap today, and he was exhausted."

Luka asked, "Where is Drew?"

Glancing up at the clock on the wall, Beth replied, "He should be…" She didn't finish before the door swung open.

Drew ushered in a tightly bound up Maggie. "Sorry we're late. The little street coming down from the school was a bit flooded."

Beth went to Maggie to help her take off her wet outer things. How Beth hated the weeks when Maggie had afternoon school instead of morning school. When winter came, the poor girl often had to walk home in the dark. Today they had decided that it was raining too hard, and Drew went to pick her up in the van.

She brushed wet curls off Maggie's face. "You ready for some dinner?" The little head nodded. After hanging up Maggie's coat, Beth began to cut some bread with the big bread knife. "Anyone else want a sandwich?" Helena and Luka shook their heads no, but she had learned that Croatians would always refuse food on the first asking, so she asked her guests twice more before they finally said that yes, they would like something to eat. Although Helena joked about losing the head of cabbage, Beth knew that her family could not afford to waste any money. The twenty-year-old girl was attending university and working as much as she could. Beth tried to spoil her as much as possible whenever she came over.

After Beth made sure everyone had food, she joined them at the table. Drew cleared his throat. "I wanted to thank you both for coming tonight." He nodded toward Helena and Luka. "We thought it best to have church on Saturday nights for now because we want you to have the option of going to church on Sunday if you choose."

Helena spoke up, "You do not have to worry about me because I will never go back."

Drew pleaded, "Helena…"

She shook her finger at him. "Do not even try. I have made my decision."

Without a trace of his typical smile, Luka said quietly, "Me too. And I know that Tanja has said the same."

With anxiety in his eyes, Drew looked over at Beth. They had talked about how they did not want to create division.

Helena leaned forward and slapped her hand on the table. "Now, I would like to learn about the Bible. Are you going to teach us?"

Drew shook his head with a smile. "Okej, okej." He opened his Bible and said, "I thought we would start in Romans. Paul uses this book to talk about the foundations of our faith, specifically our freedom from the law."

Beth was always amazed at Drew's flawless Croatian. He sounded almost native with perfect grammar and an accent to match. How did he do it?

Leaning back into his chair, Drew read the first seventeen verses of Romans 1. Then he leaned toward Maggie, who was seated next to him. "Maggsy, will you pray for us?"

Beth watched her daughter smile her biggest smile up at the dad she adored, and Beth thanked God for her husband.

Everyone bowed their heads as Maggie prayed in Croatian, "Dear God, I love you, and umm, and I think everyone here loves you. Please give Dad good words to say, and help us love you more. Amen."

Everyone else whispered amen. Beth was sure she saw tears on both of the men's cheeks.

~~~

2000: Marko:

Baka stuffed the coins into Marko's hand, muttering her order for a pack of cigarettes. After her wheezing fit the other day, he and Mama had wondered if this was it. But, of course, a week later, Baka was her old self, demanding cigarettes again. She patted his head and said, "Good boy, Petar." She had just woken up from another one of her naps and was confused. Marko ignored her and left the room to get his shoes on. Pulling off his slippers, he placed them by the door and slid on his sneakers. Mama must have heard him because she yelled out from the kitchen, "Where you going?"

He let out a larger-than-needed puff of air and dragged out his words with annoyance. "Mama, I am going to the store."

"Why?"

"*Ajme*, so I can get cigarettes for Baka."

"*Okej, okej*, go."

He pushed the door open and ran out of the apartment, down the stairwell, into the driveway, and out into the street. Ah yes, to feel the wind on his shoulders, in his breath, and underneath his feet. He was alive.

Running past Tomo, he waved a "hi" as his friend lifted up a chicken for him to see. He couldn't quite hear what Tomo was saying, but no doubt it was something about the chicken. He ran up the hilled street, turned right, and stopped in front of the Konzum. The little grocery store had the world in it: bread, chips, chocolates, gum, and Baka's cigarettes. He walked into the store out of breath, and the man at the cash register, Tomo's uncle, laughed at him. "What, Marko, did you run a marathon from Germany?"

He shook his head with a grin. "It feels like I did."

"Ha, you boys are out of shape. Tomo comes home from school every day without any breath in his lungs."

Marko looked down the first aisle of snacks. "Barba Leo, that is because we play football for a long time after school."

"My little World Cup champions."

Marko felt the grin spread across his whole face. He puffed out his chest and walked like a man. "I will be the next Davor Suker."

Tomo's uncle shook his head and laughed hard and loud, which made his large belly go in and out. "We will see about that. Right now, what do you need?"

Marko strode over to the counter like a man and plopped his coins down. "I need one pack of cigarettes for Baka."

Barba Leo grabbed a pack and handed it to Marko. "Anything else?"

Glancing in front of him, Marko saw his favorite gum, Bazooka, that he liked because of the comic strips inside. "One of these."

Barba Leo nodded, took the coins and said, "You boys need to practice harder. If you need some tips, you ask me, *okej*?"

Marko nodded and ran out of the store. In his hurry, he ran into a tall man. Marko fell back down onto the tiled floor, and the cigarettes went one way as his gum flew out of his other hand. Before he could stand up, he felt two strong hands lift him up by his arms, and he looked up into *Gospodin* Tihomir's face.

"I am so sorry." He looked down and grabbed his gum quickly.

Gospodin Tihomir took the pack of cigarettes and handed them to Marko. "It's *okej*." He smiled, slowly standing up from his crouched position next to Marko. "Why does such a small boy have cigarettes?"

Marko fumbled around with the pack. "It is for my *baka*, not for me."

The tall man nodded. "Aha, I see."

Not knowing where to look, Marko sneaked a peek at the man's face before staring back down at the ground. *Gospodin* Tihomir had weird eyes, as if they could see right through you, but then also as if they were shaking your hand and saying nice things. They were red and made Marko feel tired. He suddenly did not think he would be able to run back home.

The man turned to continue into the store, and Marko reached to pick up his gum. He was about to turn when away when for some reason he couldn't explain, Marko quickly asked the man, "Can I play with your dog sometime?"

The man tilted his head. "Why do you want to play with my dog?"

Stupid question. Yes, that's what Teacher would have said. Why did Marko say stupid things… "Ah, I… I like dogs, and I see your dog come out sometimes, and I wonder if it would be *okej* if I played with him."

Gospodin Tihomir smiled again. "Of course. You can come play anytime. But, ah, I must tell, the dog is a girl."

Marko's shoulders slouched a bit. "A girl?" He looked down at his shoes and wondered at his misfortune. "Well…"

"Her favorite thing to play with is soccer balls."

Marko's eyes leaped back up to the man's face. "Oh, well, I guess it is *okej* if it is a girl since it is a dog." He shifted his feet. "Maybe I can teach her some soccer tricks?"

"You play football?"

Marko nodded.

Gospodin Tihomir snapped his fingers. "You know, when I saw you, I thought, aha, he is a football player."

Marko felt his eyes pop out of his head. "You did?"

The man nodded. "Mmhmm. Yes, well, I better buy some bread. Come over whenever you want."

Thanking the man, Marko walked slowly and proudly back to his house. He had a dog to play with, and he looked like a football player.

~~~

1993: Tihomir

Tihomir flipped back onto his right side. He felt a touch on his left shoulder and then a murmur: "Can't sleep?"

He didn't respond, so Zrinka slid her arms beneath the sheets and around his chest. She pressed her face against his back and breathed on him. Warmth spread through his body, welcoming him home. She kissed his back and wiggled closer to him. "Tell me, my love."

The pressure was building up against his forehead. He coughed it back.

"You know that your tears never bother me."

He knew it, but still he held them back. She would not slap him against the face or yell at him for crying, he knew, but still he refused to let those tears fall. "Why, Zrinka? Why is God so far away?"

"He is here with you now."

Tihomir pushed his fist into his face. "I don't feel him at all."

"Sometimes we cannot feel him. Doesn't mean he isn't here."

"Why can't I feel him? What did I do wrong?"

Her soft-never-rough fingers traced his face. "My love, it does not mean you did something wrong."

"Well it's either my fault or God's."

Zrinka was silent and continued to brush her fingertips against his forehead, then his cheek, and then his neck. He felt his heart slow its pace as he focused only on her touch. A simple melody came from deep within her chest as she whispered the words of a song from her childhood. He let the questions fall away and focused on the words and melody of "*Kisa Pada*."

As she sang, she massaged his back, coaxing his muscles to relax. After a few songs, she let the tune fade off. He rolled over to face her and saw the outline of her face from the streetlight outside their window. "You are my life, my whole world." He leaned his forehead against her, about to kiss her, but he felt her body tense up. He drew back and asked, "What's wrong?"

"Nothing." Her voice sounded soft and small, like a mouse's.

He gently swept his thumb over her bottom lip. "You seem tense."

She closed her eyelids. "I just worry sometimes."

He wrapped his right arm around her body and drew her closer to him. "About what?"

She looked up into his eyes and touched his cheek. "I want my love to draw you closer to God."

He nodded. "And it does. You are the only thing that keeps me going, keeps me believing."

"But I shouldn't be."

His eyebrows furrowed. "Why shouldn't you be?"

Her fingers fell away from his face as she became silent.

"Zrinka." He sighed. "Think about it. First John talks about how we have not seen God, but if we love one another, his love is made perfect in us. That's what you do for me." He kissed her forehead, closed his eyes, and breathed in her smell: always lavender. She kept a small bottle of it on the bathroom sink, each morning wetting her wrists and the sections below both ears. "Your loving me is like God loving me."

She rubbed her forehead against his. "Yes, but... but I just want to make sure..."

He pulled back and looked into her eyes, which shaded by the dark. "What are you trying to tell me, Zrinka?"

"I don't know how to say it."

"Try."

"You'll take it the wrong way no matter how I word it."

"No, I won't. I promise. Just tell me."

She pulled a bit away and seemed to search the moon for answers. He waited.

"Well..." She didn't make eye contact with him. "I want to see you grow in your faith. I am sorry for you that you doubt, and I hurt with you through these hard times. But I think in these times you need to turn to God and trust him that he is always with you."

"I do try to seek God, but he just isn't there sometimes like you say he is. That's why... I have to be around you because you see him like I don't."

"I understand, but... I..." She shook her head and said in the smallest of voices, "I don't want to be your crutch."

He became silent and stared at her face. Neither of them spoke. His own mind pounded with statements, questions, his picture of her changing. He combed his hair back with his fingers. "So this is what you think of me... Weak, faithless, pathetic..."

She looked at him with wide eyes. "What?"

He sat up in the bed. "That's how you see me. You think I'm a failure in my faith."

"No, Tihomir. Listen to me..."

He shook his head and waved off her words. "No. You listen to me. I am a pastor of a church, a growing church. People respect me, and they listen to me." His fingers shook. "I give them hope, something you have... have often give me. But now... now you...you tear me down." He pushed down the tears. "You don't have faith in me."

She lightly placed her hand on his arm. "No, Tihomir, no. Please... I knew this wouldn't go well. I... I don't know how to say these things right."

Her touch was so gentle, so Zrinka. She didn't mean it... He shook his head. "No, you said it just right. You don't think I can be a pastor. You probably think my father is a better pastor." He offered a rough laugh. "Yes, better to be drunk all the time than doubt the presence of the Almighty Divine Being in heaven. Yes! That's what I'll do. I'll drink and not care about anyone but me!"

"Tihomir, please. Calm down, *ljubavi.*"

He glared down at her and ignored the fear in her eyes she seemed to be trying to hide. "You think you're so much better than me."

"Tihomir, you misunderstand."

"You think you're better than me." He laughed. "You, the one who can't have children."

She had her mouth open to speak and then closed it. She watched him for a moment. Her eyes held this look that he had never seen before. He tried to read them. Before he could identify it, she turned away from him, but not before the moonlight caught the shine of her wet cheeks.

"Zrinka..." He gently touched her back, but she didn't respond.

X

2000: Marko

Teacher called the five-minute break. It was raining again, and Marko was bored. Several of his buddies lay their heads down on their desks and closed their eyes. Marko looked to his right at Maggie. She was reading one of her books. Ripping out a clean sheet of paper, he drew a short, small line and passed it to her. She looked at the paper and then up at his face with her own face all scrunched up. Pointing to the paper, he whispered, "You don't know how to play?"

She shook her head. So he began to write down instructions, showing her how they would take turns drawing little lines and making boxes. Whoever made the most boxes won. Marko had played it often with his desk-mate in third grade, especially when the old Teacher was yelling at someone. It wasn't football, but it was a way to make time more interesting.

The two of them began to laugh quietly to themselves as they tried to beat each other. Maggie caught on quickly and almost won the first game. She did win the second game, so Marko quickly began the third game so he could show her who was the master. Neither of them had noticed that Teacher had begun speaking to the class. When Marko was about to win the third game, Teacher yelled, "What the hell is going on? This isn't *marenda*. Pay attention!"

All of a sudden, Marko realized that Teacher was standing right in front of their desk. With her thin eyebrows raised, she reached her hand out and asked for the piece of paper. Marko handed it to her. She ripped it up and threw it in the trash. Then she turned back to them and gave them both a stern look that brought their backs up straight. When she began teaching again, Marko glanced over at Maggie. She giggled quietly.

At the end of school that day, Marko was hurrying to stuff everything into his backpack when Teacher came up to him and Maggie. She set a bucket with two rags on their desk, gave them a stern look again, and then left the room. Marko threw his bag down. What great luck he had. He played a game with a girl, and now he had to miss playing football with the guys—to wash the blackboards.

He heard Maggie's voice beside him. "I'm sorry."

He turned toward her and saw her sad face. "Ah, it's *okej*." He grabbed the bucket and shuffled out the door, down the hallway, and over to the boy's bathroom. Placing the bucket in the sink, he turned the water to hot and let it fill up. Oof, but it was heavy when he tried to carry it back. He didn't let it show though and stood up tall because he didn't want Maggie to think he was some kind of weakling. He was a strong football player, after all.

When he walked into the classroom, he noticed that Maggie had pulled up their two chairs to the blackboard. He set down the water, and the two of them each took a rag, dipped it in the water, wrung it out, stepped up onto their chairs, and began to wash the large blackboards. At first, they were quiet, listening to the swish-swish of their rags. With the water, they wiped away Teacher's white scribbles. Marko did not know why the woman wrote anything on the board—her handwriting was like a complex code the class had to translate.

When the water became dark and filthy, Marko took it back down to the bathroom, emptied it, and walked back to the classroom. When he came back in, Maggie was humming a song, an unknown song to him. Probably some foreign song. But then, as she eased her rag across the board, she began to sing the words—Croatian words.

Marko set down the bucket. "What song is that?"

Stepping down off her chair, she squatted and soaked the rag in the water. Without looking up, she said, "Just a song."

He dipped his rag back in the bucket and then wrung it out. "But what's it called?"

She shrugged her shoulders.

"Well, where'd you learn it?"

Something in her eyes was deep and reminded him of Mama. "*Teta* Zrinka taught it to me—a long time ago."

Zrinka... "You mean, the woman who lives right next to you?"

She nodded.

He began to wash his side of the board. "I talked to her husband yesterday."

Her hands paused. "You did?"

"Yeah." He wiped his forehead with his arm. "He invited me to play with his dog."

She smiled. "Lipa."

"Yeah."

"I miss Lipa."

He looked over at her. "She seems like a pretty awesome dog—even though she's a girl."

Maggie threw her rag at him, and it hit him in the face.

"Hey!"

She laughed at him and then squealed and ran as he chased her. Around the room they ran as he twisted the two wet rags and tried to smack her with them. She protested and laughed and tried to convince him to stop. When they ran toward the front of the room, neither of them saw where the water had splashed over the bucket's side. They both slipped and went tumbling to the ground. They lay there laughing so hard that Marko's stomach hurt.

Who knew a punishment could be such fun.

Who knew one could have such fun with a girl.

~ ~ ~

1997: Beth

Beth placed Bruce in the stroller, buckling him in and pulling his striped hat down so it covered his ears. "My little penguin." She bent down and rubbed noses with her tightly bound up boy. "It's just you and me this morning, partner." After making sure he was safe and snug, she began to wheel the stroller out of the stairwell and outside the house.

The air was crisp, but the harsh *bura* had subsided for their short journey into town. Maggie was at school, and Drew was emailing their director back in the States about the next step they should take. He had encouraged her to go for a walk with Bruce. Drew probably needed the quiet, free of any added stress.

As Beth pushed Bruce down the sidewalk, she resisted the urge to wave to a woman they passed. When Beth had first arrived in Croatia, she had waved and smiled at people as she passed them, as she often had back in California. Zrinka had quickly informed her that strangers did not usually greet each other. She would do best to keep quiet and to herself and save social interactions for people she knew. Her advice had surprised Beth since Zrinka seemed quite the social butterfly with the way she treated everyone with the sweetest of smiles and attention that always said, "You matter to me." Nevertheless, Beth listened and kept her eyes focused ahead.

Crossing the busy street took them awhile but eventually brought them to the center of Split. Beth loved living within close proximity of the cafes, the seven-hundred-year-old cathedral, and most of all, the marketplace. Brimming over with people, food, clothes, and all kinds of merchandise, the market looked out of control. Old men and women shouted from their stands with husky voices that had been scratched raw with smoking. Customers picked their way to their desired stand, careful not to step on the discarded produce that littered the ground. The best prices were found here, outside in the pushing-and-shoving of the wind, along the busiest intersection, in the maze of living chaos: the *pazar*.

Bruce peeked his head out and studied all the tall people. Ever since winter had hit the coast, Beth had hesitated taking her baby out in the cold air. He had probably grown used to the stillness and sameness of life in the apartment. Now he leaned forward in his seat, stretching his fingers out to touch something, anything. Beth tried to keep him from stray dogs or people who were not carefully watching their steps.

She pushed the stroller down a row of vegetables and searched for some healthy looking lettuce. She drew closer to one table, and a scratchy voice said he would give her a good price of only twenty *kunas*. Beth looked up into a frowning face that spoke of age. She asked for ten *kunas*. He shook his head. Eighteen.

Beth knew a fair price was fifteen, and she would not pay a *kuna* more. Twelve.

The man threw up his hands and swore at her. Beth was not offended by the words since everyone in a given household from the toddler to the grandmother swore in every other sentence they spoke. She picked up a head of lettuce and examined it closely. She looked back at the man. His clothes hung loosely on his skinny frame. He wore a dark grey coat that bore numerous holes, as if a mouse had been eating away at it. But somehow he did not shiver like she did in her well-insulated wool coat.

He muttered that his fairest price was seventeen *kunas*.

Setting down the lettuce, she said she did not think that price was all that fair and that thirteen was the absolute highest she would go or she would find lettuce elsewhere. Before the man could respond, from his seat in the stroller Bruce let out a large belch.

Startled, Beth felt her face flush as she looked from Bruce to the man, not knowing how to respond. Bruce was staring up at the old man with a dazed half smile. The old man's eyebrows were furrowed as he stared back at the baby. Beth wondered which of the males would look away first.

And then the old man spread his mouth wide and began to chuckle. It sounded like a sort of husky "he-he-he." As he laughed, he exposed his gums, and Beth realized that he was entirely toothless. No wonder his words seemed so strangely pronounced and hard to comprehend. He left his place behind the table and came over to crouch down by Bruce. He began to talk to the baby, saying random things that Beth could not fully understand. She caught something about a wife. And a garden. He spoke softly and chatted on until suddenly Bruce reached out his little hand and touched the man's face.

The old man's eyes went wide, and he became completely still. Leaning forward, Bruce batted at the man's cheeks, which were dotted with unshaven hair. With chubby fingers, Bruce pressed against the face and let out a giggle. Leaning over the stroller, Beth watched without a clue as to what she should do. Then she saw the old man's lips tremble. He cleared his throat, but his eyes filled up just the same. Bruce laughed as his small hands became wet, as if he were playing in a puddle on the side of the road. The man reached out a shaking hand and placed it on Bruce's cheek. Struggling not to yank the hand away, Beth watched as Bruce kissed the man's hand like he sometimes kissed her face: wet and all tongue. Beth would always wipe her hand on a napkin or against her jeans. But this man just laughed and cried.

With a big toothless grin, the man stood up and shook Beth's hand with his now wet hand. He thanked her and then turned back to his table. Grabbing the head of lettuce she had picked up before, he stuffed it into a plastic bag, and, after rubbing his chin for a moment, threw in another head that looked even better. Beth reached for her purse, but the man shook his head and said that it was free. Beth protested, but the man threw his hands up in the air, signaling that he had made his decision. He handed the bag to her, patted her hand, and told her to take care of her little one. Thanking him, Beth felt her throat drying up and her eyes becoming wet. Before she could hesitate, she leaned forward and kissed the man on both cheeks. The man smiled so big, and with that, Beth said good-bye and wheeled Bruce down the row of yelling men and women who were trying to make their sales.

She breathed in deeply, wiped away some mascara that had no doubt smeared a bit, and leaned down toward Bruce. "Where should we go next, little one?"

~~~

1993: Tihomir

Tihomir walked up to the front door and opened it without knocking. "*Halo!* My friends, are you ready?"

Maggie came running out of her room. "Baba Tio!"

Swooping her up into his arms, he laughed loudly. She couldn't say "uncle" very well, so it came out sounding like she was calling him an old grandma. His name was also a hard one, but she tried her best. Hugging her tightly, he acted like she was an airplane and bobbed her around as she screamed with dozens of giggles. Beth came into the living room and with a grin watched the two of them. Maggie cried out, "Mama!" but Tihomir said she would receive no mercy. He tickled as she said, "No, no, no!" And then he let her down gently on the couch and pretended like he was going to sit on her. She scooted off the couch and shuffled to her mom, glancing back with a big smile at Tihomir. He chased her, and she went screaming into Beth's arms.

Still trying to get in a tickle here and there with Maggie, Tihomir asked Beth, "Now where is your husband?"

Beth laughed in her struggle to hold onto the squirming toddler. "I think he's still in the shower."

"Ah, such a woman, taking forever. We need to go soon."

Beth gave him that look, and Tihomir knew he should be more careful with his words. "Sorry, sorry." He had liked Beth immediately when he had met her. She wasn't afraid to say what she thought, and she wasn't about to give in to anyone else's expectations. He admired her and wished he had her courage.

"What is all this noise?" Drew entered the living room, combing his wet hair with his fingers.

Tihomir put his hands on his hips. "*Ajme*, you're slower than my *baka*, and she is dead, you know."

Drew punched him lightly on the shoulder. "Hey, I'm just trying to be fashionably late like a good Dalmatian."

Tihomir punched him back. "Ah, you American."

Beth walked over to the fridge, pulled out a container, placed it in the basket she had out on the counter, and handed it to Drew. "Put this in the car? I need to go get another blanket."

Drew started out to the car with Tihomir. "What for?"

She put one hand on her hip. "To sit on, remember? People don't want to be sitting on the grass."

On their way out, Drew said to Tihomir, "She wants this outing to go perfectly, down to the last little detail."

Opening the trunk of the van, Tihomir responded, "But this is a good thing. Your wife is exactly what we need to make this church succeed. We need someone who will take care of all these little details."

Drew put the basket in the trunk along with other items that he had placed outside: containers of food, blankets, soccer balls...

Picking up a ball, Tihomir kicked it around a bit. "Today could be the day, you know."

Drew moved things around in the back so they would fit. "The day for what?"

"The day to form a church football team."

Popping his head out, Drew grinned. "Now you're talking. We could play around today and see who would be interested."

"And then we can pick a day for us to all play." Tihomir bounced the ball on his knee. "It would be a great ministry."

"Everyone loves the game, and we could get to know the guys on a deeper level outside of church."

After closing the trunk door, Drew kicked the ball away from Tihomir. The two ran down the street, stealing the ball away from one another, pushing each other, and laughing.

Last summer during his visit, Drew had told Tihomir all about his love for football. The sport hadn't been as popular in California, focusing more on baseball and basketball. Drew's parents had placed him in a club, but he hadn't had a chance to play as much as he wanted. He had expressed his eagerness to learn from the Croatians and develop his skills. The two of them had played around a bit in the yard, and Tihomir could tell that Drew had talent.

Beth came out and called out for them to come back. Turning around, Tihomir saw Maggie shuffling behind Beth. The little girl's curls were too much for him. They bobbed around her ever-smiling face. The family had brought a movie with them called *The Little Princess*, and the girl in the movie looked a lot like Maggie. The girl also sang all the time, just like little Maggie. Tihomir had never met anyone who sang as much this little American. She was always coming up with new songs about her dolls, God, and Tihomir's dog, Lipa. Even though Tihomir did not understand half of her lyrics, he listened closely and made sure she had his full attention. Right now she was hiding behind her mom's legs, peeking out at him with a grin that said, "Come get me." Looking around as if he were studying his surroundings, he whistled his way over to her and then swung her up and around.

"Tihomir, no more goofing around. We need to leave, don't we?" Beth gave him that look again, but hidden behind it he saw a hint of playful joy.

"*Okej, okej.*" He pretended like he was going to place Maggie down on her head, and the girl squealed. He straightened her and let her down on her feet. Maggie laughed so hard she fell down on her bottom. When he picked her back up, she wrapped her arms around his neck. "I love you, Baba Tio."

He froze as she gave his cheek a wet kiss. Squeezing her tightly, Tihomir wondered at how a smile child could bring such depth and meaning to a single moment.

Drew tossed the ball into the backseat of the van, looked around, and asked, "Hey, where's Zrinka?"

"Here I am," Zrinka called out as she entered the driveway. In her hands she held a large bowl. She walked up to Beth and showed her. "*Francuska salata.* Favorite of many church people."

Beth peeked into the bowl. She smiled. "Looks delicious!

Zrinka blushed. Tihomir always enjoyed how humble and bashful his wife was. He walked over and opened the side door of the van for her. She thanked him but without looking up at him. He had decided to do everything he could to make up to her for the cruel comment he had made to her the week before. He would prove to her that he was a strong man of faith, a man worthy of her.

XI

2000: Marko

A new teacher had come to Marko's school. Marko had had the same teacher since first grade, so he was curious. What would this new teacher be like? Were all teachers the same?

As she addressed the class, Marko studied the new teacher. She was a little younger than the last one, with brown hair instead of grey. She also had a big nose. Marko found it hard to pay attention to what she was saying because all he could see was her big nose.

He felt a light kick at his shin. Glancing to his right, he mouthed a "what?"

Maggie raised her eyebrows and mouthed back, "Stop staring."

Rolling his eyes at her, he looked back up at Teacher, trying to focus on her eyes instead. They were a dark brown, like Mama's. She was talking about the last teacher, how *Gospoda* Milic—so that was her name—was pregnant and needed a break from teaching to prepare for the baby. How that woman had ever gotten married was a wonder to Marko. Did she yell at her husband all day? Would she yell at her baby?

The new teacher introduced herself as *Gospoda* Filipovic, telling them to call her that for the rest of the year. Looking around, Marko saw a similar expression on everyone's face as he had on his own: confusion. Kids had raised eyebrows and open mouths. They were to call her by her name, her actual name? They had always called the last one simply what she was: Teacher. Marko wasn't sure why, but it was just the way it was done. Now this woman wanted to change everything.

Clasping her hands together, *Gospoda* Filipovic said they would now work on Croatian. Writing on the board, she began to explain *padez* and how Croatian had seven cases, which made it hard for people from other countries to learn. Marko didn't think it was all that hard to learn. After all, Maggie seemed to be doing just fine. As she taught, *Gospoda* Filipovic spoke softly but with strength behind each word. And she acted like she actually cared about *padez*. What a strange woman.

Later on in the day, Marko and the rest of the class were working on a math assignment. *Gospoda* Filipovic had written the problems on the board, and the class was to write their answers on a sheet of paper. When they were done, she would collect their papers, and then they would discuss the answers.

One problem was really giving Marko trouble, and no matter how hard he thought, he could not come up with an answer. About to give up, he saw out of the corner of his eye *Gospoda* Filipovic approaching the desk he shared with Maggie. Bending over Maggie's work, the teacher nodded and whispered something Marko could not understand. Maggie's head popped up, her eyes wide. She said something back to the teacher that sounded like what Marko knew as "thank you" in English. He had been learning English since the first grade but still didn't know too many phrases. Most of the words he knew came from what he heard on Cartoon Network and the movies he watched with Mama and Baka. Since the movies had Croatian subtitles, he didn't learn much English from them, except for the swear words. While playing football, he and his friends would throw in some English swearing with their Croatian swearing. It made them feel tough and manly.

Marko shifted in his desk and pretended not to be listening to what the woman was saying to Maggie. So *Gospoda* Filipovic spoke English. As far as Marko knew, the last teacher hadn't spoken a word of English.

The new teacher was still talking to Maggie. Then Marko saw something incredible. *Gospoda* Filipovic *smiled*. She actually smiled at Maggie. Marko had never seen the last teacher smile at anybody, except that one time when Marko saw her at the grocery store, and she had smiled at Tomo's uncle. *Bljak*. That had been before she had gotten married. And that was a different kind of smile, one that made Marko want to throw up. *Gospoda* Filipovic smiled with a look of... kindness. Yes, that's what it was. Kindness.

As *Gospoda* Filipovic talked to Maggie, Marko returned to the problem he had been struggling over. He decided to skip it and work on the next one. Seeing that the next one was just as hard, he let out a frustrated breath. He hoped Mama would have time to do his math homework that week because these problems were hard.

Gospoda Filipovic finished her conversation with Maggie and went back to her desk. Peeking up from his work, Marko looked over at Maggie. For the love of Mary, she was smiling, too. Now everyone was all smiley and happy. What was happening to the world?

~ ~ ~

1997: Beth

Beth closed the door—quietly. Leaning against it, she listened. Nothing. Her shoulders relaxed, and she began to walk down the hallway. There it was again. Retracing her steps, she opened the door. The moonlight revealed Bruce's little face, which glistened with tears. Kneeling by his crib, she spoke softly to him and tried to coax him to sleep. He had been fussy all night, ever since dinner, and she wondered if something in his food was bothering him.

She felt his forehead again. No fever. Spoiled with two children who hardly ever fussed as babies, she was now at a loss as to how to comfort him. Zrinka had always had such a gift with children, particularly when they were upset. With a sweet melody echoing from within her, she would mend any child's woes, including Maggie's and Bruce's. Beth, on the other hand, had never been much of a singer. In church growing up, she would sing softly so that no one could really hear her. Standing next to her, Mom would sing strong, pure harmonies, which only intimidated Beth and made her sing ever more quietly. But when no one else was around, she would sing loudly and with abandon.

She smoothed Bruce's hair back away from his face and gazed into his eyes—they were looking to her for help, for comfort. There was one song—a song that often seemed to reach into her and pull out the depths of her until she felt empty. Then it would thrust something altogether different into her and fill her to the point of explosion.

Leaning closer to his crib, she began to sing softly.

"My Jesus, My Savior…"

Though the song was but a whisper from her chapped lips—a broken melody—she sang it full-heartedly to Christ and in the presence of her only son.

At first, Bruce just sat in his crib, watching her. But slowly, as the chorus faded into the second verse, he began to lie down on his side. And as she sang the chorus again, his eyes began to close and his chest began to expand with his breaths. When the chorus echoed from her lips one last time, he was already deep in his dreams. She couldn't move—the song seemed to hover in the air as she watched her little one sleep. The thought occurred to her that the last few moments were the closest she had felt to her son—and to Christ—in quite some time.

Tiptoeing out, she closed the door behind her. She looked across the hall and noticed that the light was still on in Maggie's room. Crossing the hallway, she pushed the door open a little more. Maggie lay on top of her covers with a book open on her chest. Her eyes were closed. Her mess of curls created a halo around her head, speaking of a deep and pure peace. No matter what happened each day, her children forever looked peaceful as they slept.

Beth knelt once again. She slid the book out from under Maggie's hand and looked at the cover. It wasn't just any book—it was Maggie's Bible. A children's version, it was filled with pictures of the various Biblical characters and scenes. Beth recalled a time toward the end of the war when they had been helping out at a refugee camp. Beth had been talking with a young boy when she realized that she had not seen or heard Maggie in a while. She excused herself, explaining that she would be right back. Searching around the camp, she asked Drew, Tihomir, Zrinka, and others if they knew where Maggie was. No one had seen her for a while. Beth tried not to panic. She stepped outside and called Maggie's name once, then twice. She wandered out a little farther. Then she noticed a small form at the foot of a tree. The tree was barren, stripped completely of its leaves. Rushing over, Beth scolded her, "Maggie, don't you ever run off like that again. We had no idea where you were." Maggie just looked up at her. Something in her eyes, those hazel eyes, made Beth breathe more deeply and calmed her nerves. Her heart slipped into a more normal rhythm as she bent her knees to crouch down beside her daughter. After checking the ground for insects, Beth sat down and asked, "Maggs, what are you doing out here?"

Maggie twirled a blade of grass in between her fingers. "I wanted to have time with God."

Beth stared at the five-year-old, her mouth paralyzed, words lost. Maggie just kept twirling the grass. Leaning back against the bark, Beth inhaled, exhaled. The two of them sat there for a while, quiet, looking up at the barren tree's limbs, listening to the silence, each talking to God in their own soul-filled way.

Beth had never told Maggie that she had to read the Bible. She had never told her that she needed to pray. Yet at the age of five, Maggie had known the importance of talking with God, and now at seven she was reading the Word on her own. Twice in one night, Beth was overcome with the lessons her children were teaching her.

Pulling the covers over Maggie, she kissed her on the forehead and tiptoed back out, turning off the light and leaving the door cracked open, as Maggie liked it.

She had planned on doing the dishes after she put the kids to bed. Instead, she turned on a lamp, shut off the main overhead lights, and lay down on the couch. Ever going, going, going, she now embraced the stillness, the quiet. Her body sunk deep into the couch. She gazed out at the moon. It was bright, almost full, and radiant in all its beauty. With the clouds surrounding it and covering up most of the surrounding stars, the moon was the sole performer on the night's stage.

She heard the front door open and heard his routine— shoes kicked off, coat hung up, socked footsteps approaching.

He knelt beside her and looked at her in that full way of his, embracing her before he even touched her. Then he leaned forward, kissed her cheek, and breathed her in. They stayed that way for a few moments as he entered into the stillness and quiet with her. Then he sighed and murmured, "I missed you today, especially out in that cold weather." He brushed his cold nose against her cheek and chuckled. "You know I'm only hugging you to warm myself, right?"

She couldn't help but laugh. She looked up into his eyes. "I missed you, too."

~ ~ ~

1993: Tihomir

"Here we are." Tihomir waved his hand over the scene before him. Turning the steering wheel over to his right, he drove the van off the dirt road and onto the grass. When he shifted into park, the twenty-year-old Volkswagen coughed and sputtered. Tihomir hoped it still had a few years left in it. Glancing over at Drew who was in the passenger seat, he was reminded that he still needed to find a car for the American family. They had gotten along fine walking, taking the bus, and using the van when Tihomir wasn't using it. Neither of them had complained, but he could tell that it was hard for them to adjust to. He believed that the Americans should learn to live as Croatians did as much as possible, and many of the people relied solely on public transportation. At the same time, he did not want to strain the family with more changes than they could handle at one time. He also acknowledged that Drew and Beth were not a typical Croatian couple. They both were fully engaged in ministry and trying to adapt to a culture and language utterly foreign to them while taking care of two little ones. They should have a car of their own.

Sliding out of his seat, Tihomir took a deep breath. For a moment he ignored all the sounds of the American family and Zrinka unpacking the van. Plitvice. Another place Mama had taken him as a child, the place where he first saw God. He had been eleven years old when Mama brought him and a few of his siblings to one of Croatia's most beloved national parks. The whole ride down, she had talked on and on about the big water that fell down hard from cliffs that were tall like the mountains. Tihomir hadn't been able to imagine what such a thing would look like. She had held his hand tightly despite his pleas for her to treat him like a man. Pulling and tugging at him, she had pulled him down the path, calling back every once in a while for the other children to keep up.

When they had reached the first waterfall, Tihomir took in a long breath and held it for, ah, he didn't know how long. The sound alone took over every thought he had. He felt as though it was all going to come splashing down on him and take him under. And he wanted it to. He wanted to dive in and let it swirl him about to places he had only been to in the strangest of dreams. There, amidst falls of beauty, he had seen the face of God. The big water terrified him and drew awe from him. He had heard of the miracles God had performed long ago, how people had feared the judgment, the wrath, and yet also were caught up in his grace. None of it made sense to him until that moment. To be scared but unable to run away because he simply *had* to stay. Maybe God was far more terrifyingly gorgeous than anyone had pictured him to be. He drew his first picture of God that day. Fierce eyes peering out of an enormous wave with an arm that reached out, fingers inviting.

Today he had brought his sketchbook in case he had a moment to sneak a drawing or two. Shaking his head, he tried to remember the reason for being there. A church picnic. Yes, this was a time for the congregation to enjoy a time of fellowship outside the confines of a walled-in sanctuary. He wanted to introduce them to his own sanctuary.

"Tihomir," Beth called over to him, pointing to the ground where she stood. "Is this a good spot to put our stuff down?"

Walking toward where she stood with Zrinka and Maggie, Tihomir put his hands on his hips. "Mmhmm. Yes, this is good. Close enough to see the waterfalls but not too close so that we can't hear what people are saying."

Beth nodded. "That's what I was thinking."

Zrinka was looking at him. Her eyes told him that she knew he felt at home here. He walked over to her and drew her into his arms for a hug. He breathed in her scent. Lavender. He pulled back and looked at her. "*Volim te.*"

Slowly, but most surely, she allowed a smile to cross her lips. She leaned forward, kissed his cheek, and whispered back. "*Volim tebe.*"

He felt something tugging on his pant leg. "Yes?"

A chubby little face grinned up at him. Maggie wrapped her arms around his leg, and he walked around and acted like he was trying to figure out why his leg suddenly weighed so much. She giggled and held on tighter. Lifting Maggie up into his arms, Tihomir turned, looked around, and asked Beth, "Where did Drew go?"

Beth spread out a blanket on the ground. Smoothing it out with her hands, she replied, "He went on a little walk to pray."

Why hadn't he thought of that? Tihomir was about to go join Drew when he heard a car pull up. Ivo and Sladana. Jogging over, Tihomir called, "*Halo!* How are you two doing?"

Sladana was struggling to get out of the car, so Tihomir offered his hand to help her out. She had severe arthritis, and every time he saw her, she seemed to be getting worse. She patted his hand. "Thank you, Pastor." With a kiss on his cheek, she hobbled over to the blanket with Tihomir on her arm. She made sure to yell back to her husband to hurry up, and Ivo responded with an incoherent mumble. As soon as she reached Beth and Zrinka, she let go of Tihomir and began to carry on with her favorite of friends. Tihomir watched Zrinka find a folding chair and offer it to the older woman. When Ivo came over, Tihomir suddenly thought of how that would be him and Zrinka one day. Old, struggling to move or do anything on their own. Ivo placed a hand on Sladana's shoulder, and the old woman looked up into her husband's eyes the way only a wife can. Tihomir glanced over at Zrinka. Wrinkles and arthritis were worth it.

Another car arrived, and Tihomir greeted the people. As he shook hands and kissed cheeks, Tihomir looked around for

Drew, but the American had yet to return. Tihomir wanted him to be there, to be a part of it all—their first outing. Before going off to find him, Tihomir made sure he had greeted all the people who had arrived and that Zrinka and Beth were taking care of everything, including arranging all the food the people had brought. Then he walked over to the bridge in front of the waterfall. A little ways off to his left, he saw Drew sitting under a tree with his eyes looking up to the sky. Walking over, Tihomir yelled above the roar. "Come on, Drew. The people have come."

Drew shifted his eyes to Tihomir. Slowly he rose and walked toward the bridge. When the two men were close enough to not have to shout, Tihomir asked, "Are you OK?"

Drew ran his fingers through his hair. "I can't describe it."

"What?"

Glancing toward the group of people, Drew shook his head. "I just feel like something's... wrong."

"What? Nothing's wrong, my friend. We have plenty of food, and we still have more coming. People are slowly arriving. No worries, this will be a great day."

Drew looked back to his spot at the tree. "I guess... I just have this odd feeling." He kicked a pebble into the water that rushed below the bridge. "I mean, I prayed and asked God to bless this day. But... something's not right."

Placing a hand on Drew's shoulder, Tihomir said firmly. "My friend, the enemy does not want this day to go well, so I am sure he has placed some doubts in your mind to think this first outing might not work. But do not let fear into your heart. Keep praying throughout the day, and everything will be fine." He smiled. "Sound good?"

Drew nodded. "Of course. Yes, let's get back to everybody."

The day went perfectly, better than Tihomir could have ever hoped or imagined. They had more than enough food and ate on and off all throughout the day. Tihomir and Drew formed a small football team, kicking the ball around as the woman chatted with one another and chased their children.

Once the sun began its descent, people began to say their goodbyes. They shook Tihomir's hand, kissed him, and told him what a wonderful outing it had been. Their remarks made Tihomir stand up taller with joy and satisfaction that the day had gone well. After everyone had driven away, he, Zrinka, and the American family began packing up the van. Tihomir turned to Drew and said, "You see, the day went just fine. You had nothing to worry about."

After shoving some folding chairs into the trunk, Drew stepped back and wiped his hands off on his pants. "Yeah, you're right. I guess I just worry too much."

Tihomir closed the trunk and slid into the driver's seat. As he shifted into reverse, he tried to push away the hint of doubt he saw in Drew's eyes.

XII

2000: Marko

Marko set his creation down on the desk. He wasn't sure if it was exactly what *Gospoda* Filipovic wanted and looked over at Ante's desk. That guy's model perfectly demonstrated the classroom. Ante's father was an architect and always made Ante look good with his intricate designs. Mama could not do anything like it, though she had tried. The day before she had spent hours drawing, cutting, and gluing pieces of paper to the cardboard. Oftentimes she would stand back, look at it, close her eyes as if imaging the classroom, and then get back to working on it. Baka had squawked about what a stupid assignment it was, making a model of the classroom. Marko couldn't figure it out either. He stared down at the now finished product: could Tata have done a better job?

As Marko sat down, Maggie walked up and set her own creation down, instantly making Marko feel better about his. At least his looked somewhat like the classroom. But hers? *Ajme*, it was awful. It looked like someone had thrown glue onto the whole thing. It looked like the paper desks and doors would fall over if he but blew on them. It looked like *Maggie* had made it.

He muttered, "Your parents aren't very good at artwork."

Maggie looked at him with scrunched up eyebrows. "My parents?"

Gospoda Filipovic told them all to sit down and that she would now come around and look at their classroom models. On the board she had written three math problems for them to solve while she evaluated their work. With a clipboard in one hand, she walked from desk to desk, making quiet comments to the creators. Her eyebrows rose when she saw Ante's, and she bent down to study it more closely. Marko saw her glance at Ante's face, which was beaming, and he thought he saw a question in *Gospoda* Filipovic's eyes. The question seemed to remain there as she continued on with her evaluation. Focusing his attention back onto the math problems, Marko wondered what that question was.

When *Gospoda* Filipovic came to Marko's desk, she looked at his creation, made some marks on her paper, and then moved on to Maggie's disaster. Marko peeked up to see the teacher's face. What was this? *Gospoda* Filipovic was smiling again. Why? He watched as the teacher bent down next to Maggie and said something to her in English. Maggie nodded. As *Gospoda* Filipovic stood up, she made some marks on her paper and then turned to the next. Marko's eyes caught one thing on the paper as the teacher turned: Maggie had received the highest mark, a 5.

~~~

1997: Beth

"You want any more, Maggs?" Beth lifted the pot of chicken noodle soup.

"No thanks. I'm full." Bringing her bowl to the sink, Maggie turned on the faucet to let it run for a moment as water filled up to the bowl's brim.

"Thank you, hon. You ready to go to the market?" Beth wet a napkin and wiped Bruce's face of baby food. No matter how hard she tried to get the food *in* his mouth, it somehow always ended up covering his cheeks and forehead as well as the kitchen floor.

"I guess."

"Well, go put your coat and shoes on." Lifting Bruce out of his high chair, Beth took him to her room to quickly change his diaper and put multiple layers on him. Though snow was a rare occurrence on the coast, the temperatures still descended and made layering a necessity.

"OK, let's go," Beth shouted out as she carried Bruce to the front door.

Maggie shuffled over and put her coat on. The sleeves were starting to get a little short, and Beth made a mental note to look for a decent coat that wouldn't cost too much.

With Bruce in the stroller, they set out down the street. Beth looked down at her daughter. "You didn't tell me. How was school?"

Maggie shrugged and glanced over at a stray cat on the other side of the road. It jumped up onto a dumpster and peered in. Maggie pointed. "He looks hungry."

Beth nodded. "But cats are smart. They usually find a way to get some food."

"I'm glad I don't have to look for food in the trash."

Beth laughed. "Well, I would hope you wouldn't have to."

"Mirna's family has to sometimes."

Beth slowed down her pace. "How do you know that?"

Maggie kicked an empty can across the street. "I saw them last week, after school, when it was dark."

"They were looking for food in the trash?"

Maggie nodded.

Stopping at the intersection, Beth waited for the signal to light up with a green walking man. "I'm sorry, Maggs. That's really sad."

When the light changed, the two of them crossed the street silently as Bruce peeked out of his confines at all the things around him. The baby never seemed to lack curiosity. His eyes bopped around from person to person, from the ground to the buildings to the sky.

As they entered the market, Beth asked, "Is that why you have been a little down today?"

"No."

With her free hand Beth pulled her scarf tighter around her neck. "Then what is it, Maggs?"

Maggie pulled her coat zipper up and down. "Everyone is nice to me."

Beth's forehead wrinkled. "Isn't that a good thing?"

"No. All the girls fight and get mad at each other and pick sides. No one ever fights with me. Everyone always likes me."

"But, Maggs, isn't that nice, to not fight with your friends? You're such a nice girl that everyone can't help but like you."

Throwing her hands up in the air made, Maggie look like such a Croatian. "No, Mom. That's not it." She kicked a rock down the street. You don't get it."

"Well then explain it to me."

"They don't fight with me because I am the *Amerikanka*. They like me, but I'm not one of them." Maggie raised her head, her eyes on the horizon.

Wheeling the stroller down the first row of vegetables, Beth let out a long breath and saw it appear before her, as if she was smoking. Looking down at her daughter, she noticed that Maggie's pants were a bit too short for her, the hem hovering an inch above her shoes. How could a seven-year-old verbalize so easily what Beth had been trying to figure out for herself? People had treated Beth with kindness and hospitality, but she sometimes wondered if she would ever belong. "Maybe… maybe it will get better. You know, as we are here longer. You have to remember that it's only your first year in school. It… it will get better."

Maggie shook her head, and Beth did the same. She didn't believe her own words.

"*Halo!*" A scratchy voice interrupted them.

Beth looked up to see the familiar toothless smile. "*Barba* Goran, how are you today?"

The elderly man shrugged. "Ah, you know, so-so." Crouching down, he grinned at Bruce, who was reaching out for the old man's face. *Barba* Goran let the baby slap his face with his chubby palms and pick at the hairs of his beard. After chatting a bit with Bruce, *Barba* Goran looked over at Maggie. He stood up and said, "Who is this beautiful little girl?"

Maggie stood close to Beth, hesitant to speak.

Beth spoke up, "This is my daughter, Maggie."

Barba Goran came a little closer to Maggie. "Ah, Magdalena."

Maggie smiled as she always did when someone called her Magdalena. She was proud that there was a Croatian version of her name. Beth wished there was one for her. Croatians often struggled to say "th" since the sound was nonexistent in their language. They usually called her "Bet."

The old man stretched out a gnarled hand to Maggie. Beth was unsure of how her daughter would respond, as she did not often take to strangers very well.

Tilting her head, Maggie looked up at the man's face. For a brief moment she studied it, and, seeming to have found something she liked, she reached out her hand and lightly shook the old man's hand. He smiled widely and said, "It is dear to me to meet you." Turning back to his stall, he looked around as if assessing something and then yelled over to the stall next to his: "*Ej*, Ribic! Can you borrow me your bench?"

"*Ma*, Goran, you always take my stuff."

Barba Goran waved him off. "Ah, shush up, old man. Just give me the bench."

The other man muttered something to himself but brought the bench over. *Barba* Goran grunted a thank you and carefully placed the bench next to his own. He motioned for Beth and Maggie to come sit down. "The little one has his own chair." He smiled widely at Bruce.

Beth ushered Maggie to sit down next to her. *Barba* Goran reached into his bag and took out some napkins. Placing one in front of the two of them, he then pulled out a few pieces of bread, some cheese and smoked ham and began to place them on the napkins. Beth tried her best to protest, saying they had only just eaten lunch and he should save some for himself, but it was no use. He was like a Croatian mama, ignoring any excuses, for there was never any good excuse not to eat. Besides, he, like most Croatians Beth had met, seemed to enjoying sharing what little he had.

They sat for a while and talked about everything from vegetables to Bruce's teeth that were coming in to *Barba* Goran's wife. Beth had never heard a man talk about his wife so much. Throughout the conversation she found out that his wife had died of lung cancer. Admitting that they had both smoked a lot, he shrugged his shoulders with the common expression of "What can you do?" He talked about how his wife began their garden when they first married. When he talked about the different flowers, he described them with rich detail, which retained Maggie's attention. And when he asked Maggie if she liked flowers, she told him she loved them very much. He then asked if she had ever planted any.

Looking down at her feet, Maggie replied, "*Godpoda* Kronja will not let me."

The old man's thick eyebrows furrowed. "Won't let you?"

Beth explained, "Our landlady has garden in the um, yard, and she does not like children play in it."

Barba Goran scratched his beard for a moment. Looking down at Maggie, he said with confidence. "Then you must come to my garden." He pointed to his hands. "You see, my hands give me trouble now, and my little flowers do not get the attention they deserve. Will you please help me?"

Maggie sucked in a big breath, and a smile lit up her face. "Yes. Yes, thank you so much."

The old man slapped the table. "Good. And you..." He pointed to Beth. "You must come and pick the best of my vegetables for your family."

"Oh, *Barba* Goran, thank you, but I cannot. That is too much."

He threw his hands up in the air. "I will not listen to such excuses."

Beth shook her head. He was impossible.

Barba Goran talked a bit more about the best techniques of making plants grow. Beth asked him a question about how often he watered them, and his eyebrows scrunched together as if he did not understand. Beth apologized, "I am sorry. My grammar is very bad."

Reaching over, he patted her hand. "*Ne, ne*. Croatian is hard. You speak very good. I am an old man, and I do not hear so good." His smile comforted her and made her feel like he'd just called her the most beautiful woman in the world.

When they had thanked him and stood up to leave, he gave them some cabbage and carrots and, of course, would not let them pay for any of it. They said their goodbyes and began their walk back home. Maggie tugged on Beth's coat, and Beth looked down. "I like him, Mom."

"So do I."

"He makes me feel not so different."

"Me, too, Maggsy."

~~~

1993: Tihomir

Tihomir plopped down at the kitchen table. "*Ajme*."

Drew nodded. "I love church, but I'm tired."

They had only just walked in the door, but somehow Zrinka already had coffee in Tihomir's hands. As she turned back to the counter, he caught her arm to thank her. She flinched. He let go of her arm as well as his words of gratitude. His touch had not been as gentle as he had meant. Wanting to apologize, he at the same time did not want to make a scene in front of Drew and his family. He would make sure to explain it to her later.

He looked across the table at Maggie, who was sitting in Drew's lap. "How did you like church, Megi?" The three-year-old never seemed to notice the different way he said her name.

She tilted her head at him, giggled, and then hid her face in her father's arms. She didn't seem to like to talk much.

He leaned forward. "Megi, will you sing for me?"

The curly head popped up. Maggie sat up in Drew's arms and began to sing about her newest doll that her grandmother had sent her, whom she had named Funny. The entirety of the song all sounded like nonsense to him, but he leaned back in his chair and laughed good and hard. In the middle of her song, Maggie let out a yelp. Lipa, Tihomir's dog, had come up to the little girl and given her hand a nice slobbery kiss. Maggie squealed with delight, slid off Drew's lap, and threw her hands around Lipa's neck. When the dog proceeded to lick Maggie's face, Tihomir laughed at Beth's horrified face. Beth had been helping Zrinka with lunch, and she had turned around to watch the interaction between her daughter and the dog. Tihomir patted the dog's head. "Do not worry, Beth. Lipa is merely greeting Maggie with the traditional Croatian kiss."

Beth's glare made him try to hide his laugh with his hand. He called Lipa to him, and the dog came bounding over with Maggie chasing after him. Tihomir rubbed the dog behind her ears as she stared up at him with big eyes, one of them blue and other brown. Tihomir had thought her eye color strange until his brother, Neno, told him that the two eyes colors were common with Dalmatians. Now Tihomir thought the color combination to be beautiful.

Maggie was trying to climb on Lipa's back for what Drew called a "piggy-back ride." Tihomir pulled her up into his lap and began his ritual of tickling her. Beth came over with a trying-to-be-stern face. "Lunch is ready, you two."

Tihomir grinned up at her. "*Yup!*"

"*Yup!*" Maggie echoed.

After Zrinka and Beth served everyone, the two families sat down at the table. Zrinka glanced over at Drew and asked, "Drew, would you to pray for us?" Nodding, Drew bowed his head and prayed over the food and over each of them.

Why did she ask Drew to pray? Tihomir was the man of the house. He was the pastor of the church. Did Zrinka doubt his faith that much? When Drew said "amen," Tihomir looked up at Zrinka and caught her eye. She tilted her head as if she did not know why he was looking at her that way. Shaking his head, he looked down at his plate and began to eat some of the rice. He realized that Beth was saying something about *Gospodin* Kronja, the American family's landlord. She was cutting the chicken into small pieces for Maggie. Handing Maggie a piece, she commented, "He's such a nice man. Both him and his wife have helped us with anything we've needed."

Drew added, "Last Saturday they invited us upstairs for lunch. We were up there for hours, and Maggie fell asleep in my arms." He looked over at his daughter, who was sitting in Beth's lap, stretching out her toward another piece of chicken. Then he looked up at his wife. "Hey, we should have them over for a meal sometime."

Tihomir nodded. "Ah, very good idea. You know, I am so happy to see you are getting along with them."

Beth spoke up, "I just wish that the rest of the neighborhood was so accepting."

Drew turned to her, "What do you mean?"

Beth gave Maggie a fork to stab the chicken pieces with. "I don't think it's a secret of how cold some people are to us."

Drew shrugged. "I think people are pretty nice."

"Nice, yes. But they always look at me as if I'm from Mars."

Zrinka touched Beth's hand gently. "I think I know what you mean, Beth. It is very little, not so easy to see, but still very there. You must to understand. This neighborhood is one small village, and they all move together to here." She motioned toward Tihomir. "When we move here, they look at Tihomir like he is, uh, from Mars, yes?" She was blushing slightly. Tihomir loved how hard she tried to practice English. "He is from North, and even me, I am from Dalmatia but not their village. Every person who is not one of them is strange to them because they all grow up together and no other people come here." She stroked Maggie's hair. "Some people do not like different things, different people. But we must try to help them see different can be very good. They need to see God who live in us."

Beth squeezed Zrinka's hand. "Thank you." She let go and smoothed some loose curls back off her forehead. "You're right. It will get better. It just takes time. But we'll get there." A gentle smile crossed her face, and she turned to help Maggie, who seemed to be getting chicken all over the place, except, of course, inside her mouth.

The conversation continued on, but Tihomir's thoughts remained on what Zrinka had said. All his life he had been different. His father had been a pastor, not a priest. Even in the North, that was a very *different* thing. Now he was a pastor. And working with Americans. He looked over at Maggie's little face that her mother was trying to keep clean. Would the neighborhood accept her? Would such an innocent child prepare the way for them similar to how John the Baptist had for Jesus? Tihomir swallowed some spinach and wondered if Maggie would make them all a little less different.

XIII

1997: Beth

Beth refilled everyone's cups with coffee. Smiling at all the faces, she could not believe how many people now came to the weekly Bible study. Every couch was filled to busting, every folding chair occupied, and every space on the floor taken (though Beth had made sure to find cushions for people to sit on since cold floors practically equaled death). How many people would show up the next morning to hear Tihomir preach? Beth scolded herself for wondering such a thing. Her hope was not for people to leave that church and come to their home. She prayed for unity. But was it a possibility anymore?

Drew was wrapping up the evening: "Thank you all for coming tonight. It's amazing that we have this many people with the *bura* raging outside." Beth could hear the wind slamming against the house in its fury. Sitting down next to Drew, she relaxed in the fact that the wind was powerless to hurt anyone inside. Croatian houses were built well, and hardly any damage was ever done.

Clearing his throat, Drew leaned forward and interlaced his fingers. "Does anyone have any prayer requests or praises this week?"

Helena mentioned that her mother's health was getting worse. Luka expressed a concern for a coworker's marriage. Tanja asked for prayer for her brother who would soon need to serve two years in the army. Ivo shared that Sladana's arthritis was starting to keep her from fulfilling simple daily tasks. Looking across the room at Ivo, Beth noticed the dark circles under his eyes, the fidgeting of his hands, and the absence of his smile. He seemed lost without his wife. In fact, when Beth thought about it, she could not think of a time when she had not seen the two side-by-side. Sladana was a fiery sort of person. Fueling Ivo with her energy and passion, she also added life and zeal to the group's time together. Beth missed having her as Sladana always had some strong words of encouragement to offer Beth. Ivo cleared his throat and, shifting in his chair, said firmly, "But God is good."

Drew nodded. "Yes. No matter how confused, alone, or lost we may feel, God is constant. He is good." He made eye contact with Ivo. "It is hard sometimes to believe it though."

The old man sat up taller. "Doesn't make it any less true."

With a grin, Drew replied, "No, it doesn't." Several others shared various needs as well as some praises for the good God had been doing their lives. Once most everyone had shared, Drew leaned forward in his seat asked people to bow their heads. He thanked God for the time they all had shared, thanked the Holy Spirit for being among them, and asked for each person's request. He ended by asking for strength and courage for all of them as they went about their week. "Amen."

It was not until two hours later that people began to slowly trickle out. They loved to stay and chat and drink more coffee and eat the chocolate chip cookies Beth had made. It seemed that each time they came together, another woman asked her for the "American cookie" recipe. As the people started to make their way out the door, Beth shook their hands and kissed their cheeks.

When they had all left, she walked over to the couch where Maggie and Bruce had both fallen asleep. The two siblings were snuggled up against one another, his head on her shoulder, and her head on his head, both their mouths open in a light snore. Kneeling in front of them, Beth gently tipped Maggie's head the other way and then scooped Bruce into her arms. He fidgeted around for a moment and then relaxed against her, his soft breath on her neck. She carried him down the hallway and into his room, settling him down into his crib. Returning for Maggie, Beth lifted her up with a little more difficulty. Though Maggie was fairly skinny and light, she was nonetheless a seven-year-old.

Once she had both kids tucked in, Beth returned to the kitchen and began to wash the mugs they had used. She was reaching for the drying towel when she heard a knock on the front door. Drew was out driving some of the people home who did not have a car. Beth did not have to open the door though because *Gospodin* Kronja swung it open. It was his way: knock on the door while opening it, never fully giving Beth warning as to the landlord's coming. Biting back a smile, she turned to greet him. "Good evening. How are you, *Gospodin* Kronja?"

He muttered a "just fine" before sitting down at her kitchen table. When he motioned for her to join him, she asked him if he wanted any coffee. Her offer was met with a shake of his head. Pulling out a chair for herself, she noticed that his frown seemed deeper than usual.

He tapped his finger on the table for a while and then stared out the window, which was nothing but black since it was eleven o'clock at night and the clouds were covering up any hint of moon or stars. Finally he shook his head. "Too many people."

Beth leaned forward. "Sorry?"

He motioned toward all the folding chairs. "Every Saturday night you have all these people over and throughout the week you have people come in and out, letting the cold wind into our stairwell. And…" He paused and lifted his hands in the air. "It would not be as big of problem if you were throwing parties and this was all for fun." Smacking his lips, he shook his head again. "But I hear strange songs, more people come every week, and the neighbors are starting to ask questions."

Glancing at the clock, Beth prayed for Drew to come back soon. "What they to say?"

He brushed some crumbs off the table. "They say you are a *kult*."

Beth wanted to reach for the dictionary that was propping the door open. Surely it did not mean...

He turned to look at her. "When you first come here, you say you are working with humanitarian organization, yes? And I know you are working in some church with Tihomir." He pointed to his left, where Tihomir's house stood. "Fine, I do not ask questions. But now you have church *here*." He stared at her. "That is not *okej*." Letting out a deep breath, he sighed. "Now please listen, you and Drew, you are good people. I like you very much. But I have lived with these neighbors all my life, and they are my family. I do not want people saying things about my choice of renters. Such a thing could hurt my wife and me." He looked at her with the saddest of eyes. "I am sorry." Standing up, he walked toward the door and then turned back to her. "Tell Drew that I give you to the end of the month and then you need to find a new place." He walked out, slamming the door behind him.

After a few minutes, Beth sat still, listening to the tick of the grandfather clock, staring into her empty cup. She got up and poured herself another cup of coffee. Setting it down on the table, she struggled to steady her shaking hands before she spilled the hot liquid. She sat there, sipping at her coffee and nibbling at a cookie until Drew came home. While taking off his coat, he began telling her about how Ivo had asked him the funniest thing about how...

"Beth, are you all right?"

Out of her peripheral view, she saw Drew standing there, watching her. She did not look up. "*Gospodin* Kronja is kicking us out."

"What?" He came to her and sat down next to her. Cocking his head to the right, he gently touched her cheek.

"Bethy, your face is so white. What did you say about *Gospodin* Kronja?"

"The whole neighborhood thinks we're a cult, and such gossip will hurt his reputation, so he's kicking us out."

Drew sat back in his chair and stared at the floor.

Beth realized that coffee did not seem appealing with her stomach churning. Standing up, she walked over to the sink and emptied her cup. "That's it, I guess."

Drew looked up at her. "What do you mean?"

Shrugging her shoulders, she reached for a sponge and began scrubbing the mug. "We've tried our best here. We tried to work alongside a Croatian pastor, but then confrontation ended that, and then we tried a church at home, and now apparently we're a cult. I can't seem to learn the language to suit anyone, and Maggie says she will never fit in."

"Maggie's been completely fine here."

"Show's what you know."

He stood up next to her. "What are you saying?"

She grabbed the drying towel and began to dry off all the mugs she had washed earlier. "I'm saying that it's time to leave."

"Leave?" She had turned her back to him, but she knew he was staring at her. "Leave? So we need to find another place to live. We can do that. But Beth, all our work has not been for nothing. Look at me." He gently touched her arm and turned her toward him. "People might look at us weird and say things about us. But remember all the bodies that filled those chairs." He pointed toward where the group had gathered an hour ago. "Did you look into their eyes tonight? There was hope. These people have gone through a war and poverty and then all the drama in the church. Now they have hope. God is working here. And sure, it might be hard, but these people are worth it all."

Beth felt a tingle down her arms, but she ignored it. "What about us? What about your family?" She pulled away from him and continued drying and putting away the dishes.

"I don't know what you're talking about. We've been happy here."

She stared at him. "Who's we? Have you heard me ever say that I'm happy here?"

"Just the other day you said how much you enjoyed meeting that sweet old man at the market. Didn't that make you the least bit happy?"

She didn't answer him.

"Is everything so horrible here?" He touched the small of her back, leaned in, and rested his chin on her shoulder. He murmured, "Bethy, I've seen you with these people." His breath on her neck was soft, like Bruce's had been as she carried him. "You love them. I am so, so sorry about the hard things that have happened and that now we have to find a new place. I want more than anything to give you a perfect world." He tilted her chin so she would look at him. But this is where God has called us, and I would hate to be anywhere else."

Leaning into him helped her avoid eye contact with him. She wanted to, but did not, whisper back, "I just wish I felt as sure as you do."

~~~

2000: Marko

Marko kicked the crushed-up can as he walked alongside Tomo. Neither of them had said a word yet. Though they had never discussed it, they had a tradition of not saying a single word until they got over the hill to *Barba* Leo's store. Then they would rush in and begin asking Tomo's uncle about the freshly made pastries he had for sale that day. This morning like any other, the only sound to be heard as they walked up the hill was that of the coins jingling in their pockets. Their mamas always gave them enough for a pastry for breakfast and for a snack at *marenda*. Marko and Tomo usually bought their *marenda* snack in the morning so they could play football during the thirty-minute rest from books without interruption.

Huffing up the hill that seemed even bigger than Tomo's father, they raced each other to the store. Marko won, of course, because his legs were longer and faster than Tomo's. His friend ran too much like his chickens: taking small strides and with little form. Once they arrived, they entered the store, greeted *Barba* Leo, and began to look through the glass and lick their lips. The floury, sugary pieces of heaven seemed to be calling out for them to buy a pastry, or two. They quickly called out their choices to *Barba* Leo.

Marko did not have to think very long about what to buy for a snack. He almost always got a bag of *smoki*. Mama hated both the smell and the orange tint it left on his fingers and face, but he thought it was perfectly heavenly. Mary, the mother of God, probably bought a bag of it every day for Jesus when he went to school. With the bag in one hand, Marko grabbed a 0.25-liter Fanta with the other.

Paying for their treats, the two boys stuffed the bags and drinks into their backpacks. Then, with a good-bye to *Barba* Leo, the two of them walked up the second hill, which was tiny compared to the first one. The hard part this time was carrying not only the several heavy textbooks but also the food and drinks. As the straps tugged against his shoulders, Marko pretended he was playing in the World Cup and had been unfairly injured by an opposing Brazilian player. He would never allow such a small thing as Pain to stop him. He would get that ball and make it go toward the goal. He would get up this hill.

When they arrived at the school, they sat down on the broken steps in front and began to eat their delicious pastries. The jelly in Marko's poured forth and smattered his face. Thank God Mama was not here to fuss over him and try to wipe it all off his face. The two boys sat in perfect peace as kids ran about them, eating, talking, playing *lastrika* and other games… Maggie walked past them and joined the girls playing *lastrika*. Tomo turned to Marko, "What is it like?"

Marko licked his lips and turned to Tomo. "Ha?"

Tomo pointed his pastry at Maggie. "What is it like to share a desk with *her*?"

Shrugging his shoulders, Marko looked at his pastry. He was trying to decide if she should eat the outside first and leave the rest of the jelly center for last. "She is a girl. She can be annoying."

"No, I mean because she is an *Amerikanka*."

"So?"

Tomo took a large bite of his pastry and wiped his powdered-sugar-covered hand on his pants. "My mama says they are a bunch of heathens."

There was that word again. "What does heathen mean?"

"I don't know... something bad. Mama says they don't believe in Mary."

Both boys crossed themselves as they had seen adults do.

Marko glanced toward where Maggie was playing *lastrika*. "Well, the girls like her. She can't be so horrible."

Tomo wiped his hand on his face, leaving a streak of white. "Girls are blind... like Mateo."

"Mateo?"

"My blind rooster. He got into a bad fight with Petar."

With a shake of his head, Marko took his last bite as the teachers began to call them inside. The two boys stood up and tossed any trash they had onto the ground since the trash can was too far away. They walked into the classroom and counted down the minutes until *marenda*.

During one of the five-minute breaks, Marko drew a picture of a man, an older version of himself, kicking a soccer ball into a net. As he tried to make sure that the black shapes on the ball were perfect, he realized how hard it was to draw a soccer ball. Sometime he would have to study the ball he had at home and see how he could draw it better.

"That looks very nice."

He turned to see Maggie looking at his drawing. He had forgotten that she was still sitting next to him. Crushing up the paper in his hands, he threw it on the ground and muttered, "It's a piece of *govno*."

Bending down, Maggie picked up the wadded up paper and gently unfolded it on her desk. With her pencil, she wrote something on the bottom right hand corner. With a proud smile on her face, she smoothed out the wrinkles and nodded. Leaning over, Marko saw that she had written his name in the corner in nice letters, much nicer than his own. Maggie pointed to the paper. "Can I keep it?"

"Why the hell would you want it?"

"It might be worth something someday."

Rolling his eyes at her, he turned back to face *Gospoda* Filipovic as she began talking to them about nouns. Out of the corner of his eye, he saw Maggie carefully place his drawing in between the pages of her textbook. He hoped she would not notice, but he was sitting up taller and thinking about buying a sketchpad.

~~~

1993: Tihomir

Tihomir reached out his arms to little Maggie. "We're going to have lots of fun tonight, aren't we?" She clapped her hands and shook her head left to right excitedly. Beth bent down to Maggie's level and explained, as Tihomir had seen her do many times, that if Maggie wanted to say yes, she should shake her head up and down, and if she wanted to say no, she should shake her head left to right. Beth kept demonstrating, but Maggie's focus had shifted, and she was looking at a bird that had just flown to the window. The three-year-old pulled away from her mother and ran over to the couch, climbed up, and looked out the window at the bird. Tihomir held his hand over his mouth to hold back his laughter. "Well, you tried."

Sighing, Beth put her hands on her knees and stood up. "You sure you two are going to be all right?"

He batted the air with his hand. "Ah, do not worry. We will play with Lipa, draw some pictures, and maybe take some *rakija* to Zrinka for her stomach pains."

He had correctly predicted that Beth's hands would fly up to her hips. "Tihomir, my baby girl will not have anything to do with any alcohol, you hear me?"

Drew entered the room, "Who's having alcohol?"

"Maggie and I." Tihomir crossed his legs and grinned.

Drew nodded. "Oh OK. So I fixed the carburetor, and it all looks fine now. I think we're all set to go."

Beth looked over at her husband and seemed to study him with a hint of a smile in the corner of her lips. "Hmm dearest, would you like to wash up a bit first?"

"Huh?" Drew turned to Tihomir. "Am I dirty or something?"

Tihomir shrugged his shoulders. "You look *okej* to me."

Beth gave Tihomir her best attempt at a glare. "You men are hopeless." She shook her head and left the room with the two men grinning.

Drew swooped Maggie up despite her squeals and gave her a raspberry kiss on her stomach. Then he dropped her on Tihomir's lap. "Take care of this little monkey." The men laughed as Maggie made sounds like a monkey, crawled down off Tihomir, and began walking on all fours. "Have we told you that her favorite movie is *Jungle Book*?" At that, Maggie began to ask for "Junga Book! Junga Book!" Walking toward the door, Drew waved back at Tihomir, "Have fun!"

Tihomir yelled a "*bog!*" to him and then scooped up the squirming monkey. "We are going to do something better than watching a movie."

"What, Baba Cestin?"

"Would you like to learn how to draw a monkey?"

She bobbed up and down on his lap. "Yes, yes, yes!"

Carrying her upside down with her yelping away, Tihomir walked over to his bookcase and pulled out his sketchpad. Then he grabbed a few pencils from his desk that sat in the corner of the living room. He plopped Maggie down on the wood floor and showed her his tools. Maggie took the sketchbook in her hands and began to flip through it. The monkey seemed to calm a bit as she gazed at each of the pictures. Halfway through the notebook, she pointed excitedly. "Me! It's me!" The first week the American family had arrived, Tihomir had drawn Maggie helping her mom unpack by carrying small items to the rooms Beth pointed out. The process had taken quite a while because Maggie would often get distracted by something exciting—like an ant on the floor or a stuffed animal that had been packed away for the last couple of weeks. In the drawing, Maggie was tightly hugging a stuffed fox, a package of paper towels discarded on the floor.

Maggie brought the sketchpad over to Tihomir and pointed at the pencils. She looked up at him with her hazel eyes. "Teach me." The pastor of a church and the son of a pastor opened the notebook to a fresh page, handed the little girl a pencil, and thought of a verse he had not fully understood before: "Let the little children come to me, and do not hinder them, for the kingdom of God belongs to such as these."

The two of them spent the rest of the evening drawing and eating and laughing. Since Zrinka was sick in bed, Tihomir sliced up some cheese, *prsut*, and bread for them to munch on throughout the night. At one point in the evening, little Maggie was attempting to sketch Lipa, but the dog was failing miserably as a model. She could not seem to sit still for more than a minute at a time. Tihomir would have given up quickly, but the child sat patiently and kept working. She would draw a few lines, then look up, and gently command Lipa not to move. While her drawing hardly resembled a dog, Tihomir had never seen such dedication and perseverance. When it came to heart, Maggie was a supreme artist.

Looking up, Maggie asked for another sandwich. Popping it into her mouth, she drew for a moment and then looked back up at him. "What is wong with Teta Zwinka?"

The little one was still struggling with her r's, and Tihomir had to hide a smile. "Her stomach is hurting very much, and she needs to sleep."

A bunch of the crazy brown curls fell onto the left side of her face. "Her tummy hurts because a baby is inside?"

Tihomir reached to make up another sandwich for himself. He had put plates of all the fixings on the coffee table in the living room so that they would not have to get up for food. "No." He concentrated on the number of slices of cheese he wanted in his sandwich. "No, there is no baby inside."

"Oh." Maggie tilted her head. "Maybe I ask God?"

"Ask God what?"

"For a baby."

But such prayers were never answered. God remained silent. The Drava River was quiet. The skies were still devoid of any promise. He, a pastor, could offer his wife no comfort or hope. Yet maybe the fault lay with him, with the way he prayed, with his unbelief. Perhaps if this angelic cherub whispered her own pleas, God would be merciful and listen. "Yes, my little Magdalena, ask God."

XIV

2000: Marko

Marko sat down on the sidewalk in front of *Barba* Leo's store. He was glad Mama wasn't there to yell at him not to sit on the cold ground because, if he does, as she always said, he will get sick and die. He had done it many times and was still alive, so to *pakao* with that nonsense. Pulling his notebook for math out of his backpack, he flipped to a blank page. After he had hunted through his pencil case for the perfect, sharpened pencil, he sat and stared at the page. What could he draw? He thought of something, but it would be difficult to draw. It would probably look like nothing more than a small child's drawing. Even so, with the pencil's tip on the paper, he began to draw a set of trees on both the left and right side of the paper.

Marjan. His father had taken him bike riding there that last summer before he went back to the war for the final time. That day his father pedaled his big bike with Marko holding on tightly behind him. His father pedaled harder and harder as they went, making wind that blew into Marko's face, grabbed his breath, and pulled his hair straight back. That was his dad: the Wind-maker. He would make such a wind that it would blow them down the path between the big, tall trees. The large trees rose up high to the heavens with their branches and then fell deeply to the ground with their shadows. The two of them rode on the flying bike until they reached the playground, where many kids were swinging or riding down the huge slides—at least they seemed huge back then. Then his father got off the bike, plopped Marko on the ground, and pulled a ball out of the backpack Marko had been wearing. They kicked around the ball until they got really hot and sweaty, and then they jumped into the cool sea. His father didn't waste a single minute. He asked Marko to come close to him.

"Listen, son, right now you swim like a little puppy, but to be a strong Dalmatian man, you need to swim right. *Okej?*"

Marko nodded as his father showed him how to kick his feet hard just beneath the surface of the water. Then he showed him how to sweep his arms up past the top of his head and then down to his sides. They did that for hours until Marko's little body was limp and his fingers wrinkled like his clothes before Mama ironed them. Picking him up into his arms, Tata had carried him back to the bike, set him on it, and then walked it slowly to the car. Marko asked him to make wind for him, but Mama had brainwashed even Tata: he said that the cold air would make Marko's wet body sick and then he would die. Marko didn't know what the old man was talking about. It was still plenty warm out. But his father didn't listen. He just whistled along with the birds up in the tall trees.

Now in between the two rows of trees on his paper, Marko drew a bike with a man and a little boy on it. He struggled with drawing the bike and thought about how when he got home, he would pull out his father's bike from underneath the stairwell. Then he could sketch it. And maybe even ride it. He had grown a great deal in the past five years.

At the top of the page he drew the park and the water. He was starting to get frustrated when a shadow fell on his page. He looked up.

Gospodin Tihomir.

The man smiled and said, "Hello again."

"Hello."

Gospodin Tihomir sat down on the sidewalk next to Marko. Perhaps Mama was mistaken and the cold ground did not affect men but only women and little girls.

"You never came to play with my dog."

Marko had wanted to, but he hadn't known how to go about it. What was he supposed to do? Knock on the door of the heathen's home and ask to play with their dog?

"Yes, I'm sorry. I have been busy."

The man pointed to Marko's paper. "You have some skill with that."

Marko covered it with his hands. "Ah, it's just a piece of *govno*."

Shaking his head, the man stretched out his legs in front of him. "My first drawings weren't the best. Nobody draws perfectly the first time. But they still aren't pieces of *govno*. They're just the beginning of something better."

Marko's hands relaxed. "You draw?"

"Yes, since I was a little bit younger than you." He peeked over at Marko's drawing. "Marjan?"

Marko stared down at his paper. How had he known?

"It's my favorite place to draw." He pointed at the sides. "Especially the trees."

"The bike is too hard."

"Well, let's think about a bike for a minute." The man began to talk with his hands and then stood up to demonstrate the various features of a bike. While he was talking, Marko noticed something under the man's eyes: dark half-moons that sat above his cheeks and drew his eyes down. Did being a heathen make him look like that? He shuddered. But Maggie didn't have those dark moons. Maybe it was something that came later on in life when one became an adult. He realized that he should have been listening to *Gospodin* Tihomir. As the man talked and motioned, Marko began to draw on a new page a bike without any passengers. After a few minutes, the man sat down next to him, not hovering over him but giving him time to sketch. *Gospodin* Tihomir began to whistle, and the two of them sat like that for a couple hours with only a few words exchanged about how the bike could be improved.

After he had drawn countless bikes, Marko looked up and noticed that the sun had begun to set. Mama would not be happy that he had been gone so long and had not eaten anything. He began to stuff his notebook into his backpack. "I must go."

Gospodin Tihomir slowly stood up and brushed the dirt off his pants. "Thank you for showing me your drawings."

Marko grinned. "Thank you for teaching me."

The man ruffled Marko's hair. "Anytime. Seriously. And you can come play with Lipa whenever you want."

"I will." Marko turned to leave.

"Wait."

He turned around, and *Gospodin* Tihomir laid a strong hand on his shoulder. The tired look in the man's eyes faded away and was replaced by a light, a fire. With a voice as quiet as a mouse but as strong as a tiger, *Gospodin* Tihomir said, "Don't give up, son."

Marko was not sure he understood, but something about the man's words dove deep within him, as if a treasure to be later discovered. He nodded.

Gospodin Tihomir patted him on the shoulder. "Good boy." There was something else in the man's eyes that Marko could not name. Something sad. Something empty. Could emptiness fill something to the point where nothing else could be present? Could emptiness be an actual presence? He suddenly thought of the man at the cemetery, the one who was missing a leg, the one with eyes that stared.

Marko offered an awkward smile and a "good night" and then turned to walk home. The whole way back his mind overflowed with bikes and dogs and football—and what it meant to be a man.

~~~

1993: Tihomir

Tihomir tiptoed into the dark room, slowly closing the door behind him so it wouldn't creak or whine. Then he crept over to his side of the bed.

"Tihomir?"

His arms fell to his sides. He whispered, "Ah, darling, I'm sorry. I was trying not to wake you." He slid off his slippers. "Go back to sleep."

He heard Zrinka turn over under the layers of blankets. "It's *okej*. I was already awake. Now please, go sleep on the couch. I don't want you getting sick."

Slipping under the covers, Tihomir searched for her face until his hand could rest on her cheek. "In sickness and in health… my place is with you."

With the moonlight shining through the bedroom window, he saw a smile spread across her face. "You don't have to take everything so literally."

With his index finger he traced her face, something he often did in an attempt to commit her face to memory—every line, every little curve. Her forehead was hot at his touch, and his finger picked up some of her sweat. He remembered something she used to tell him about sweat.

Their dearest memories were formed at their favorite place, Marjan, where they would run and race each other in between the tall trees that hovered above them. Sometimes when the wind pushed through and rustled the leaves, the trees seemed to be cheering the two of them on. She would arrive first at the playground, as she always did, and be swinging on that old swing that creaked as she went back and forth. As she curled her legs beneath her and then stretched them out in front of her, she would tip her head back and grin at him. With a frown he would ask, "How come I'm soaked and you don't have a drop of sweat on you?" She would shake her black curls and laugh. "Tihomir, Tihomir, don't you know? Girls don't sweat."

Now her face was dripping as it often did when she got sick like this. She had already been sick five times that year, whether with the flu, a cold, various infections…

"Did Maggie leave?"

He played with one of her curls, twisting it around his finger. "Yes, love. Drew just picked her up."

"She really adores you."

"She adores you more. I tried to sing to her today and she pressed her hand against my mouth and told me to stop."

Zrinka laughed. There was nothing like making her laugh, so he told her another story, and she laughed even harder, which triggered a coughing spasm. She coughed long and hard, struggling to breathe. Holding her tightly, he rubbed her back as the cough racked her body. Once it passed, she was wheezing and seemed to crumble into him. He stroked her hair and whispered, "Beth is concerned about you."

He knew she couldn't respond yet, so he continued to rub her back and let the silence take over. After a few moments, he felt her body relax against him, and he continued hesitantly. "She really wants you to see a doctor."

More silence.

"We were talking about this new hospital that opened up in Zagreb. As soon as you are better, you and I could take a little trip up there."

He felt her head shake back and forth.

"I'm just asking you to think about it…"

She let out a raspy "no."

"Zrinka…"

"Tihomir…" She took in a deep, long breath. "I am done with doctors."

"But this new hospital has an incredible team of doctors who have studied around the world…"

She touched his lips. "*Dragi*, thank you for caring about me. I know you want to help me." She touched the scruff on his chin that showed that he hadn't shaved in a few days. "I have no more energy for doctors." He thought he heard a smile in her voice. She murmured, "I trust that God will care for me."

He peered at her face and tried to make out the expression there. "God will care for you? We have left a lot to God that he hasn't even touched."

She whispered, "That's not true."

"Well, what has he done to help you? Every year you catch whatever sickness is going around the neighborhood. You want me to watch you slowly grow weaker and weaker just like I did with..." He gritted his teeth in an attempt to catch hold of his emotions before they ran out of his control.

Zrinka pressed her hand against his chest. "Tiho, I am sorry that my sickness reminds you of your sister. I am sorry that I can offer you no comfort. But you need to recognize that this is a different situation."

"What is so different? You are sick. Ana was sick. You will not let me take you to anymore doctors, and my dad refused to spend money on a doctor for his own daughter." He realized he was yelling and wanted to apologize, but he could not get the right words out.

"You just said the difference. I am a grown woman, and I make the decision of whether to go to the doctor or not. Your dad made a horrible choice for a little girl who could not make the decision for herself." She paused and reached up to touch his face. "Tihomir, you are not your father."

"Stop it!" He sat up. "What do you know about me? You think I am this good person? I am not. I am just as bad as my father."

She tried to sit up but couldn't. "That is not true. You are a completely different man. Can you not see that? God has done so much both in you and through you."

"Do not talk to me about God."

"Why are you turning away from him?"

"See? I am just like my father. Preaching and pretending like I believe in someone that I do not believe in!"

She tried to touch his hand, but he pulled away. "I know your heart, *dragi*. This is not who you are. It is who you think you are. I think you believe in God a whole lot more than you do."

"Stop it! What do you know about faith? You pray to a God who has not given you anything you have asked for. You ask for children, and nothing. You ask to just be well and be able to do ministry, for *him*, and nothing. Your faith has achieved nothing for you."

She shook her head. "You are wrong. My faith gives me the strength I need."

"Strength? Woman, look at you. You are weak. You do nothing. Your life has no purpose right now."

She shrank back from him.

"Zrinka, that is not what I meant. Let us forget all this." He reached out for her. "Please, come close to me."

She turned away from him. "Tihomir, please go sleep on the couch. I do not want to get you sick."

He tried to turn her back to face him. "It does not matter. I do not care if I get sick. I just want to be close to you. I need you."

Her voice was faint. "I am so tired, love. I feel like I have nothing to give you."

"You do not have to make love to me. I just want to be close to you, to hear you breathe, and trace your face." He touched her forehead and kissed it. He felt her trembling. "What is wrong?"

Her voice trembled along with her body. "Sometimes… your love scares me."

"What is that supposed to mean?"

"Tihomir, I love you, but I feel like the more you doubt God, the more you use me as…"

"As a what?"

"As a replacement."

He laughed. "You think you are like my God or something? You think because you are such a righteous woman that you are something to be worshipped? I will tell you what you are." He knew he should stop before the words came flying out. "You are a barren woman, always sick, and cannot even make love to her husband. You are pathetic."

He immediately wanted to grab the words and shove them back. The two were still, staring at one another. She didn't say anything. She didn't cry. She just lay there before him, silent. Only silence.

Her eyes stared out at him, reminding him of the eyes of the refugee children he had helped the other day. He and Drew had gone to one of the nearby refugee camps to distribute clothes and food from a humanitarian organization. One of the children had come up to Tihomir and looked up at him with wide eyes that held a mixture of desperation and longing. That child had looked to him for help, for needs to be fulfilled. Zrinka now looked at him, needing him to be the strong man he used to be, yet he could not do anything for either of them.

Getting up from their bed, he left the room and strode out of the house, without a shirt and without any shoes. Slowly he began to jog and then run and then sprint as a lamppost lit his way down the middle of the street. His bare feet pummeled the ground as he created a rhythm with his steps and breaths. With each step, he pushed himself harder and harder, hoping that he could run away from himself.

~ ~ ~

1997: Beth

Beth woke up to a strange sound. Trying to bring herself out of the fog of sleep, she sought to identify the sound. Was someone coughing?

Bruce. He had had a hard time falling asleep, struggling against her as she held him and coughing as she laid him down. Now at—she looked over at the clock beside her— four in the morning, he seemed to be at it again. Glancing over at the form next to her, she noted that Drew was in a deep sleep, his arm laying across his face. She pulled the covers off herself and searched the floor for her slippers. Some of the women in the church had made each of the Austins a pair of slippers for the family's first winter in Croatia. The wool was scratchy and hot, but Beth wore them because the kind, old women had hand-knitted them just for her and her family.

After tiptoeing into the hallway, she flipped on the light switch—and then groaned inwardly. Still no power. They had been working on the power lines in the neighborhood all weekend. It reminded her of when they had first come to Split, and they only had power for a few hours a day because of the electricity rations. Over the past couple years, she had become accustomed to having power all the time. She felt her way to the kitchen and searched the drawers for a flashlight. Once she found one, she clicked it on. Thankfully the batteries in it were still good. Tiptoeing her way to Bruce's room, she slowly opened the door and shined the light into his crib. He sat there, his face pale and wet, his forehead shiny. His breathing was labored and when he coughed, it sounded different, almost like... the bark of a seal. That thought triggered something in her brain, though she wasn't awake enough to remember what it was.

Picking him up, she tried to calm him down by talking to him in a soft, quiet voice, but he could not seem to stop coughing. "Bruce, Bruce, baby, honey, it's OK, it's OK." She rocked him as she hastened over to the living room to where the bookcase stood. With one hand holding Bruce, she used the other hand to shine the light on the books until she found the large one she was looking for. Putting the flashlight in her teeth, she grabbed the book and sat down on the tiled floor. She tried to flip to the right page while also trying to calm Bruce down.

She heard Drew's voice behind her. "Is he OK?"

She took the flashlight out of her mouth. "I've heard this kind of cough before. I just can't remember what it means." She flipped to the section she was searching for. "Croup."

Drew came over and sat beside her, taking the flashlight from her and shining it on the pages. "You think he has croup?"

"His cough sounds like a seal barking. That's a common thing with croup. Some of the nurses I worked with in Sacramento told me about the babies that came in with it."

"What can we do to help him?"

Beth scanned the page. "We need a vaporizer or a hot steamy shower."

"But the power's out."

She rocked Bruce lightly. "When do you think it'll be back on?"

She could feel his eyes on her. "I don't know, Bethy." He leaned over to glance at the book. "Is there anything else can do?"

She was the nurse. She should know what to do. She kept trying to read, kept looking for an answer. "I... I don't know what to do." This was all Luka's fault. He had come over the other night for Bible study. His face had been shiny with fever, and he had held Bruce and kissed him on the cheek, like people often did. Now her baby was sick.

Drew's voice was steady. "Let's take him to the hospital."

"Mom?"

Drew shone the light on Maggie, her face pale. Her curls spun around her wide eyes. "What's wrong?"

Beth stood up and shifted Bruce to her other hip. "Your brother's sick. We're going to the hospital."

Drew crossed the room, picked Maggie up, and led them to the car out front. The wind swooped around them, nearly knocking them down. Drew set Maggie down in the back and held the door open for Beth. She sat in the back with Bruce on her lap as he began to cry. Within a minute, Drew was speeding down the moonlit street.

Beth had never been to the ER there and didn't know what to expect. When they arrived, they walked into the waiting room and looked around. The room was dimly lit and not a person in sight. Shifting Bruce to her other hip, Beth thought that this was a good thing since it meant that no other patients were waiting. Drew set Maggie down, and for the first time, Beth realized that they were all still in their pajamas.

They looked around until they saw a door with some light showing from underneath. They knocked and heard a voice yell out "Yes?" They opened the door and there sat a middle aged, heavyset woman wearing blue scrubs. She looked them up and down, sighed, and signaled them over to the examining table. Beth assumed she was a doctor although she never actually introduced herself.

The woman asked Bruce, who was still crying, "What's wrong with you?" Before Beth could reply, the woman had taken Bruce from her hands and put him on the examination table. Bruce began to scream. Beth reached out for him, but the woman waved her away. After a moment, without looking at Beth, the woman asked for his birth date.

That's right. They hadn't filled out any paperwork. "October 20, 1996. His name is…"

The woman scribbled the date on a piece of paper and returned to examining him. That's when Beth looked at the woman's hands. No gloves.

No washing of hands.

Beth looked bewilderedly at Drew, who was sitting with Maggie in his lap. Drew sat still and quiet with a hint of uneasiness. He had always hated hospitals. Maggie also sat quietly, her eyes fixed on her baby brother.

Standing beside the table, Beth tried to stay out of the woman's way. "Excuse me, what you think he has?"

Silent, the woman took off Bruce's diaper and stuck a large thermometer in his rectum, waited a few minutes, pulled the thermometer out, and made a "tsk-tsk" sound with her tongue.

"What is his…" Beth tried to think. "Temperature?" She said the word in English, hoping it was something similar in Croatian.

The woman responded, "Too big." She then inserted something else into his rectum.

"Excuse me, what is that?"

Bruce was howling and trying to tear away, but the woman kept a firm hold on him with her left hand. Quickly, she inserted an IV into Bruce's chubby little hand.

Beth tried once more, "What you give him?"

The woman finally looked up, irritated. "*Adrenalin.*"

Adrenaline? Was the word that similar in Croatian? Why adrenaline? She wanted to ask so many questions and tried to think how to phrase them. Would they admit him and put him in a vaporized tent? Would they let her stay with him?

The woman pulled the IV out, slapped a Band-Aid on it, and handed Bruce to Beth.

Beth stood there, unmoving. The woman motioned to Bruce. "Take him home."

"But..." Beth held Bruce as he continued to scream. She spoke in English, "You're not going to admit him, put him in a tent, do something?"

The woman collected her paperwork. "No problem. He'll be fine soon. This will all pass." She nodded and ushered them out. Drew stood up with Maggie in his arms, his face covered with confusion.

Beth continued to protest, but the woman simply led them out of the room and walked off to another room. Beth called after her, "Wait! Please!"

The two of them stood together in the waiting room, each one holding a child, as Bruce continued to scream and lash around in Beth's arms. She stood, watching Drew's face. Doctors and nurses shuffled passed them, not noticing this small family. A door opened and cold air filtered into the strongly heated room. Drew came closer to her. She began to speak, "I..."

He shook his head. "It's OK, Bethy."

She stared at him and saw something she had never seen in his eyes before. What was the word?

He took another step closer to her. "It's time."

She gazed at him, unsure.

He pressed his forehead to hers and whispered again, "It's time." He held her, Bruce, and Maggie. "Time to go home."

XV

2000: Marko

Thunder rumbled against the classroom walls and was followed by lightning that lit up the cloudy world outside. All Marko could think was *no football today*. He slumped down in his seat as Teacher, that is *Gospoda* Filipovic, tried to keep their attention on the board, where she was writing out in chalk about the different kinds of weather. As he attempted to keep his eyes focused on the board, he realized that at this point, the last teacher would have been yelling at them and calling them stupid for not paying attention. *Gospoda* Filipovic sometimes got a very serious look on her face, and her voice would get firm in a way that meant no nonsense, but she never yelled. Why was that?

At the end of the day, everyone began to pack up their things as *Gospoda* Filipovic went around and made sure that everyone had some kind of jacket or an umbrella to shield them from the rain. Since Marko did not have either of those, he grabbed his backpack and soccer ball and snuck out of the classroom before she saw him. When he reached outside, he saw that the rain had collected and filled the front part of the school so that he was sure to get his shoes soaked. Mama was going to be angry.

Maggie ran past him and into a car that had pulled right up to where he stood. The car began to pull away and then stopped. It backed up, and Maggie climbed out and ran to him. Holding the hood of her jacket tight around her face, she told him, "My mom wants to know if you want a ride."

Shifting his feet, Marko looked around. "Ah, no." He passed his soccer ball from one hand to the other. "No, I am *okej*."

She looked at him like he was a small child. "It's raining real hard."

Thunder grumbled all around them and followed up closely with lightning. Marko shrugged and tried to look like he did not care. "I will be *okej*."

Maggie glanced back to the car. Turning back to him, she said, "Listen, my mom will not let you walk home in this."

He looked down at his shoes, trying to decide.

Maggie continued, "Trust me, if I go back to the car and tell her you said no, she will probably come out and carry you into the car." She smirked.

Marko threw up his hands. "Ah, *okej*."

He followed her to the car, wondering what Mama would be more upset about: his shoes getting wet or his riding in the car with heathens. Then again, she would not have to know about his getting a ride with them. If his shoes got wet, she would know for sure.

When he climbed into the backseat of the car, he settled in next to Maggie's younger brother. The little kid's eyes were stuck on the ball in Marko's hands. Maggie's mom turned around and smiled widely at him. "Oh, I am so glad. I did not want you to walk in this horrible rain."

He shifted in his seat. He suddenly wished he had walked home. Unsure of what to say, he tried in English, "Thank you very much."

Maggie's mom nodded. "You're very welcome. What's your name?"

"Marko."

She turned back to face the front of the car and began to pull out of the school. Switching back to Croatian, she said, "Nice to meet you, Marko. Please put on your seatbelt."

Looking over at Maggie, Marko saw how she had buckled herself in. He had hardly ever worn a seatbelt. The back seat of their old Yugo did not even have seatbelts, and with both Mama and Baka in the car, he hardly ever sat in front. The American's car, on the other hand, which was a big van, had the same kind of belt in the back seat that was in the front seat. Pulling the belt over his shoulder, he hooked it into the part by his hip. The little boy next to him was fastened into something even worse, a whole seat of its own. Maybe heathens were more worried about dying in a car accident because they didn't know about heaven.

"So what did you two learn about in school today?"

Marko glanced at Maggie, who began to talk about precipitation and the other processes of weather they had learned about. How she could remember all those details was amazing to him. She sounded like she could reteach it all to the class tomorrow! As her mom asked questions, and Maggie answered them, he also noticed that Maggie's Croatian seemed better than her mom's. The American woman seemed to struggle with certain words and had more of an accent. How could that be? Weren't grownups supposed to be smarter than kids?

Maggie's mom looked at Marko in the rearview mirror. Then she glanced down at the soccer ball he had in his lap. "Do you normally play football after school?"

Marko nodded.

"You play well?"

He shrugged.

She turned down a street. "Maggie's dad keeps saying that he needs to kick a ball around with Bruce. Does your dad play with you a lot?"

He pulled the seatbelt away from his chest, but as soon as he moved his hand, it fell right back against him. "Ah, he used to."

Maggie looked over at him. "But not anymore?"

"Ah well..." He shuffled the ball between his hands. "He died."

The American woman's eyes darted back up to meet his in the rearview mirror. The van was filled with silence. Then she said to him, "I'm sorry."

There was something in her eyes that bothered him, that made him want to cry. He wished she would not look at him like that but would just look away.

As the van moved slowly down the street, Bruce looked up at Marko and then at the ball in his lap. Reaching out for the ball, the little boy looked up again at Marko with big, wide eyes. Marko handed it over to him and watched as Bruce threw it up a bit into the air, watched it carefully with his eyes, and then laughed as the ball landed in his lap. Maggie looked at Marko and shook her head. She seemed to be thinking the same thing he was: what a strange kid. He seemed so happy, so content just throwing a ball in the air.

Maggie's mother asked, "Where do you live, Marko?"

Marko looked at the houses outside the car. He pointed to the right. "Turn in here, and that is our apartment."

As Maggie's mom turned the wheel, she said, "Well, it was nice to meet you, Marko."

Marko nodded and turned toward Bruce, extending his hand. The kid hesitated and then placed the ball in Marko's hand. The little boy's face now slumped down into the saddest face Marko had ever seen. Suddenly Marko wanted out of the car before the kid started crying. Within a few seconds, however, Bruce had picked up a book that had been wedged in between the seats and had started flipping through it and looking at the pictures. Once more his face was covered with a grin, his eyes lit up.

When the car came to a stop, Marko quickly unhooked the seatbelt, said good-bye and then darted out the door and into the stairwell of his apartment. Jogging up the stairs, he shook out his hair, which had gotten a little wet in just the seconds it took him to get from the car to the front door. When he walked into their apartment, he immediately heard his mom yell, "Are you wet?"

"No, Mama!"

He took off his shoes that had barely gotten damp and went to the kitchen to steal a piece of bread. As he thought about the car ride, he realized that the only thing he found wrong with the heathens was that they were overly happy.

~ ~ ~

1997: Beth

Beth gently placed the cookie sheet onto the second rack of the oven. Since Tanja and Maggie had been working hard for the past hour, Beth wanted to give them a treat. And chocolate chip cookies seemed like the perfect thing. Tanja always went crazy over the American chocolate cookies, especially when they were fresh from the oven: gooey with melted chocolate that could burn the roof of one's mouth.

Beth snuck a peek at the two of them working at the kitchen table. With her elbows on the table, Tanja was leaning over the textbook and pointing to various images and words while speaking enthusiastically to Maggie. Despite Tanja's effort, a permanent frown painted Maggie's lips. She wouldn't even glance up at Tanja. Beth had thought that the news of their moving back to America would make Maggie happy. Hadn't she said herself that she could never fit in here? Wouldn't she be much happier in the States? One time Maggie had told her about how she wanted to have her own farm in America and ride horses all day. Beth had already thought of a place in California where Maggie could take horseback riding lessons. In America, Maggie would have many more opportunities than she had now in Croatia.

With the tips of her fingers, Beth swept some crumbs from off the counter into her palm and brushed them off into the trash. Even Bruce, who would normally be crawling around the place and eating things off the floor, was now pulling on her pant leg and crying. When she tried to pick him up, he pulled away from her, so she would set him down, and then he would begin tugging on her and crying again. The tension in the apartment seemed to be affecting his mood. Beth picked him up again despite his pushing away from her and crying. Taking the pacifier from where it had been on top of the refrigerator, she plopped it into his mouth. He spit it back out. Tanja and Maggie were now watching, so Beth took Bruce to his room and put him in his crib. He was probably just tired. But as soon as she laid him down, he began screaming.

Reaching her hand over the railing, she stroked back the curls from his forehead. "What do you want, Bruce? Darling, I don't know what you want." She tried to sing to him one of the songs Zrinka would sing, but he kept wailing, his eyes growing redder and wetter. Walking over to the closet, she opened it and grabbed a few toys. One by one, she handed the toys to him, only to watch him throw them onto the floor. She had tried feeding him, changing him, and yet none of it seemed to calm him down. The day after they had taken to the hospital, the electricity had come back on, and they had been able to give him a hot, steamy bath, and his fever had gone down after a couple days. Within a few more, he was back to normal. Yet now, two weeks later, he was a mess, continually fussy, and nothing seemed to calm him down or make him happy.

She continued to try different things until, finally, little by little, he exhausted himself. His cries grew soft, his eyes grew heavy, and at last, he fell asleep. Sitting on the floor for a while, she leaned against the crib and watched him sleep on his back, his little arms up beside his head. She felt like taking a nap as well.

"Beth?"

At the sound of Tanja's voice, Beth kissed Bruce on the head and left the room on tiptoe, carefully shutting the door behind her. Entering the kitchen, she noticed that Maggie had fully slumped down in her chair with her gaze on the tiled floor. Tanja's eyes met Beth's. "I think we are done for today."

Maggie looked up at Beth for a moment with a question in her eyes. Beth nodded. "Yes, you can go play. Bruce is sleeping, so make sure you're not too loud." Without a sound, Maggie left the room and went down the hallway. Beth watched her walk away and then asked Tanja to check on the cookies while she went to talk to Maggie for a minute.

Cracking the bedroom door, Beth peaked in. Maggie was perched at the top of the bed, looking at her reflection in the mirror and studying it. Entering in, Beth whispered, "I see a beautiful girl." She sat down on the bed behind her daughter. To Beth's surprise, Maggie turned around and wrapped her arms around Beth. For a few moments, the only sound in the room was Beth's fingers stroking the tangled curls on the little girl's head. Since Maggie loathed having her hair brushed, Beth sometimes let it run wild rather than fight with it. The crazy curls were growing longer every month, which drove Beth crazy but made Drew happy. He had always loved how long and curly Maggie's hair was and often said that it was the hair of a princess. Sometimes, after dinner, Drew would swoop Maggie up into his arms and call her his little princess. Beth would just stand back and smile and think that there was nothing quite like watching the two of them together. Stroking her daughter's hair, Beth whispered, "Princess Maggie."

The small girl in her arms drew back, her large hazel eyes peering up at Beth. Multiple questions layered those eyes and called up to Beth for help. Smoothing curls off Maggie's forehead, Beth asked her, "What is it, Maggie? What's wrong?"

"Mom," Maggie murmured, "I don't fit in."

Beth nodded. "I know, hon. That's why moving back to the States will be a good thing. You will be surrounded by other American girls who understand you."

Maggie shook her head. "I won't fit in America."

"Why do you say that?"

"I'm not American."

"Of course you are. You were born in America."

"No." Maggie turned and looked back in the mirror.

Beth looked around the small room. Before they had moved to Croatia, they had had a nice, three bedroom house. Maggie's room in that house had been about twice the size of the one she had now. "Do you want to stay here?"

"If we go to America, I'll never see Petra again."

Beth played with one of Maggie's curls, twisting it around her index finger. "She's your best friend, isn't she?"

Maggie nodded. "Like *Teta* Zrinka."

Beth paused. "What?"

"*Teta* Zrinka is your best friend."

Letting go of Maggie's curl, she let it fall onto the girl's left shoulder. "Yes. She…" Beth looked at both of their reflections in the mirror. "You'll make new friends in America."

Maggie turned back to her. "What about Barba Goran from the *pazar*? Who will visit him and help him in his garden?"

Beth tucked a loose curl behind Maggie's ear. "We only just met him a little while ago."

Maggie's eyes held something intense, something Beth could not identify. "But he asked me to help him."

"Maggs, you will have so many opportunities in America that you'd never have here."

Turning away again, Maggie lay down on her stomach.

Palms pressed down, Beth smoothed out the comforter on Maggie's bed. "You've never really liked it here, so I…"

"Can I have some time alone?"

Beth reached out to touch Maggie's shoulder to turn her back around. That's what Mom would have done. Back in their house in Michigan, Mom would come into Beth's room and press her for more information on whatever was bothering her. Mom had never understood that her pressing had only resulted in pushing Beth further away. Yes. Maggie needed space. Beth sat back and said, "OK. I'll let you be." Sliding off the bed, she stood up and walked to the door. Pausing, she turned back and asked, "Do you want a cookie?"

Her eyes to the wall, Maggie shook her head.

Heading back to the kitchen, Beth noticed that Tanja had scraped off all the cookies onto a large plate that had red and green trim around the rim. If Beth remembered correctly, underneath the layers of gooey delight lay some kind of Christmas scene or greeting. The plate had been a gift from Beth's mother last Christmas, along with a coffee mug and an apron. Now that Christmas was nearing, Beth needed to find that apron so she could wear it while baking. Unless they left before Christmas. She ached to be back with family for the holiday, but Drew felt like that might be rushing it.

Beth sat down at the table and chuckled. "Excited for a certain holiday, are we?"

Tanja grinned back up at her and then raised her hands in the air. "Oh, I forgot an important American tradition." She reached down into the small fridge and pulled out a one-liter carton of milk. Turning back around, the smiled. "Milk and cookies." After filling two cups, she set them on the table, and the two women enjoyed dipping their cookies into the milk and taking big bites. They laughed at each other as milk and melted chocolate dripped from their lips and chins.

After they had each had a few cookies, Tanja reached a hand across the table to touch Beth's arm. "*Okej*, now you tell me what is wrong with Maggie."

With a glance toward the hallway, Beth let out a big breath. "I'm trying to figure her out. I thought she was unhappy here. She told me the other day that she feels like she'll never fit in. It's not that kids don't like her or don't get along with her. It's that she will never be one of them. You know?"

"Yes. Poor girl." Tanja traced the rim of her glass with her finger. "So she is not happy because she cannot fit in here?"

"That doesn't seem to be what's troubling her today. See, we told her yesterday about a big decision Drew and I have made."

Tanja leaned forward. "What kind of decision?"

Since Beth hadn't told anyone yet, she played with a cookie, breaking it into pieces before popping them into her mouth. Mom had never liked the routine and had many times told Beth that she was only making a mess. But Beth liked to savor each bite, taking her time and relishing the flavors. She cleared her throat. "Well, Tanja... we're moving back to America."

Tanja slowly leaned back and then shifted her gaze away from Beth to somewhere on the table beside the plate of cookies. The two women had eaten most of the right side, so now they could see a jolly Santa face with the words "Ho, ho!" drawn near the top of his head.

Beth sipped on her milk and tried to interpret the look on Tanja's face.

Now it was Tanja's turn to clear her throat, her eyes still looking away. "So. You are abandoning us."

"What? No, we love you and we want to be here with you." Beth reached out to touch Tanja's arm. "It's just that with

Bruce's experience in the ER and the landlord kicking us out and my struggling with the language and everything else, I just don't think this is where we're supposed to be."

Now Tanja looked up and met Beth's eyes. "What about us? Tihomir went crazy and now you are crazy too."

"That's not fair."

"It is the same thing."

Beth sat back in her chair. "How is it the same?"

Standing up, Tanja took her purse from the table and slung it over her shoulder. "For Tihomir and for you, the problem is that you try to tell God what is the right thing for you to do and then you ignore his voice."

"How can you say that I am ignoring God's voice?" Beth stood and began clearing the table. "I've been talking to God about all this." She dumped the two empty cups into the sink. "I read the Bible. I pray every day."

Tanja looked at her with brown eyes that were growing wet and red. She whispered, "But are you listening?"

Silence followed Tanja's question, the two women stood in the kitchen, looking at one another, waiting, wondering. But soon the sound of Bruce's crying began. Beth wiped her hands on a dishtowel. "I need to go check on him."

Tanja nodded. "I must go too. I need to get home to my family."

Beth hung up the dishtowel on a hook above the sink. "I'll see you later."

Tanja murmured a good-bye and then walked down the hallway and out the front door.

Leaving the dishes, Beth walked down the other hallway that led to the bedrooms. When she reached the door to Bruce's room, she stopped and leaned against the wall. It was cool on her back and brought shivers down her arms. Sliding down the wall, she crouched and hugged her knees. Bruce's cries were growing louder. She tried to listen, but she couldn't hear anything else.

~~~

1993: Tihomir

Tihomir sat in the front row, next to Maggie, who was struggling to sit still. Beth had been reluctant to let Maggie sit up there with him since the child rarely managed to sit still for more than a few minutes, but Tihomir had insisted that Maggie would be his *sreca*, his luck. He would need her since Zrinka was at home, sick with a cold. He had never preached a sermon without his wife there listening and silently praying for him. As he thumbed through his notes, he noticed that his fingers shook lightly. He tried to keep them still, tried to clench them into a fist, but still they trembled. He didn't know why he was so nervous when it was supposed to be just a short sermon, allowing more time that morning for the worship. He was wondering this when he felt a tug on his sleeve. Maggie was looking up at him and giving him one of her wide grins. And in that brief moment, his tremors eased, and his heart began to slow until it reached a steady beat. He bent his head down and kissed her lightly on the top of her head. Somehow at her young age, she knew he needed to be encouraged and knew just how to brighten his spirits. It was in this that she reminded him of Zrinka with her quiet joy and soft love.

The two of them sat side-by-side as Drew gave the announcements. The American's Croatian impressed Tihomir. Along with decent vocabulary and grammar, Drew had mastered the Dalmatian art of waving one's hands about as he spoke. Even now, as he talked about the small group on Tuesday nights, he was waving his hands about enthusiastically. His vigor was contagious, and Tihomir hoped that the whole congregation would be infected with it.

When Drew had finished, Tihomir winked at Maggie and whispered to her, "Save my seat."

Standing up, he walked to the front of the room and shook Drew's hand. He quietly thanked his friend and then and set up his notes and Bible on the music stand. He closed his eyes for a brief second, and focused on his breathing, making each one full and deep. He coached himself, reminding himself that this is what he was born to do. Opening his eyes, he nodded and extended his hands out. "Unity." He let the word ring out and linger in the room. "Unity is what we need, what Paul instructs us in Ephesians four to focus on developing. It is here that he addresses the church in Ephesus, much as I am addressing you now." He paused and smiled as heard the rustling of pages—a signal that many people had brought their Bibles. Good, good.

He continued, "Paul begins by telling the believers that they need to be humble and gentle. You might ask, how can we be humble and gentle? Well, Paul answers that question for us." Clearing his throat, he read from the marked page in his Bible. "Verse two reads 'Be patient with each other, making allowance for each other's faults because of your love.' You see, it is in relationship that we learn to be humble and gentle. And it is in relationship that we learn about unity, and where is unity most needed than in the church?" Tihomir stepped out from behind the music stand. "Unity means that instead of becoming irritated and frustrated with each other, we choose patience."

He grinned. "I know. I know. Patience is not our favorite word. But it is such a key concept. Instead of reacting with anger, hatred, or bitterness, we should hold back and choose something far stronger: love." He walked back to the music stand and picked up his Bible so that he could walk around with it. Zrinka had always teased him about this habit. Whenever he preached, he struggled to stay in the same place but instead would often pace or roam around the room as he spoke.

"Paul continues in verse eleven by listing all the different gifts, and the various responsibilities, the church has: prophecy, evangelism, teaching..." He walked down the aisle between the rows of chairs, pausing at each row and motioning to people. "See, we each have a gift. Each of us has something specific to offer." He motioned to Biserka. "Biserka, as we all know, makes the best palacinke, no?" Smiles and nods spread throughout the room since most of them had tasted and enjoyed her homemade crepes. "It may seem simple, but she had blessed many and has been able to minister to their hearts while she fills their stomachs." The older woman blushed and swatted away his compliment.

He grinned and motioned to Zlatko. "And Zlatko can fix almost any problem you have in your home—plumbing, electrical... he can do it all!" Zlatko shook his head as his face spread out into a wide grin.

Tihomir continued, "We all have different talents, and no matter how small they might seem, they are important." He let his smile fade and grew serious so as to emphasize his following words. "But... but what is the point of that gift, that talent, if we do not use it for the good of the church? You see, the church *cannot* function as individuals. We need to work together because then, and only then, can we do great things."

He paused and walked over to where Maggie was sitting. Softening his tone, he gestured toward her. "I asked the children to stay with us this morning instead of going to Sunday School. Why? To demonstrate that we need them too." He waved across the congregation. "Every child in this room, every adult, every person, has a gift that the church needs, whether it is teaching, encouraging, serving… We need them. And they need us."

He flipped his Bible open again. "Verse sixteen says, 'As each part does its own special work, it helps the other parts grow, so that the whole body is healthy and growing and full of love.' " He paused and took a moment to glance out at and make eye contact with each of the thirty or forty people. Except for a few squirming kids, most of them now looked up at him, waiting for him to speak. "Growth happens when we each do what we need to do and then help others in their giftings. We have gone through a lot as a church and as a people." He motioned to the cross at the front of the church and then to the flag on the right side of the room. "But together we can rise out of this. With our hearts full of love and our hands ready to work, we can grow and flourish."

Flipping back the pages of his Bible, he continued, "Paul also states in Romans chapter five, verses four through five, 'The strength to go on produces character. Character produces hope. And hope will never let us down.' No matter how hard things get…" He looked out at them and then noticed an empty chair in the front row. He walked over to it and then stood up on it. It created the effect he desired: now every single pair of eyes was on him. He emphasized each word: "I say, no matter how hard things get, we will go on, and we will have hope."

For a moment, all was silent. They were all gazing up at him, and he back at them. Then applause filled the room and grew as he stepped down and took his seat again next to Maggie. He squeezed her little hand, and she squeezed back. Yes, she was indeed his lucky charm.

As the applause died down, two of the church's young people walked to the front. They had begun leading the congregation in worship a few weeks before. They were still young in their faith, and their music skills were still developing, but their hearts were pure and passionate. Tanja sang while Luka strummed on a guitar alongside her. Although Luka was pretty shy and did not look up very often, Tanja closed her eyes and sang loudly and powerfully.

See, this is what he had been talking about in his sermon. These two brought what talents they had to the church in humility and grace. Tihomir believed that they would help lead the church and move it forward. Bursting with joy, Tihomir sang along and encouraged Maggie to clap her hands. She tried her best to smack her palms together and ended up doing more laughing than clapping. Her little girl laughter reflected the happiness he felt. With music pouring from his lips, he celebrated having delivered an effective sermon, the tremor in his hands forgotten. He glanced around the room, and he could see it on people's faces: he had given them hope.

XVI

1997: Beth

Beth rocked Bruce in her arms as she shuffled into the backyard, whispering to him about how the sun had come out that day and how the wind had calmed to a light rustle. Every day he still seemed overly restless and fussy, no matter what they tried, but for a moment he was calm, just like the wind, and he began to fall asleep in her arms.

She heard someone call her name softly. Zrinka. Walking over to her left, Beth stopped at the waist-high stone wall that separated the two houses. Zrinka stood there, her hands clasped together. Reaching out, Beth laid one hand on Zrinka's and looked around. "Is Tihomir home?"

Zrinka shook her head and pointed to Bruce. "How is he? I hear about what happened."

Shifting him to face Zrinka, Beth watched as Bruce's eyes slowly opened and peered up at Zrinka. He immediately reached out to Zrinka.

Beth handed him over and then stretched out her arms that were aching from holding him. "He's doing well. He recovers pretty quickly from these things. He was crawling around yesterday, trying to catch a lizard."

A smile spread widely over Zrinka's face. She seemed to get thinner every time Beth saw her. Looking up at Beth, Zrinka asked, "And you? You are well also?"

Beth picked at a flower that was growing through the cracks of the wall. It had always been something that puzzled her. How could something grow among rocks? She murmured, "I'm OK."

And with those words, she experienced something she often had over the years—Zrinka remained quiet, but her eyes remained steady, waiting, and seeing through the barriers Beth was trying to put up. With her gaze dropped downward, Beth traced the cracks of the wall with her fingers. Then in the silence between them, she whispered, "We're leaving."

Nodding, Zrinka returned her gaze to Bruce's face. "I was think you do this."

Beth tipped her head. "Really?"

Zrinka lifted a finger to tickle Bruce. He caught onto it and wrapped his fingers around it. "I had fear in my heart about this."

"Why?"

Zrinka tickled Bruce, and he let out a giggle. "I see every day a little more how all this is unhappy to you. You want children is happy, but you does not think it can be. You try to have church, but then there is problems too big."

Beth leaned against the wall. "I just don't think I can handle it."

Shifting her gaze back to Beth, Zrinka reached out with her free hand. With a touch ever so gentle, Zrinka rested her hand on Beth's arm. And with a voice barely above a whisper yet somehow stronger than a battle cry, Zrinka said, "You does not have to handle."

Beth nodded. "Thank you, my friend." She exhaled. "I was afraid you would judge me for leaving, but you understand, don't you, that it's too much for me, for all of us?"

Zrinka's gaze remained steady, and her words remained weighty. "You misunderstand. You do not have to handle because is not your job to handle."

Beth nodded again. "Yes, I know. I don't have to deal with this because it is too much for me. I can go back to the States."

Zrinka shook her head. "No." Her gaze became intense, penetrating. "When you come here to our country, you try do everything, handle everything, in your strength. Now you see you cannot handle everything. Why? Why can you not?" Zrinka's tan face was engulfed in a grin of joy. "Because is God's job to handle."

The two women stood there under the sun and in the cool breeze, with Zrinka bouncing Bruce on her hip, and the baby boy giggling and reaching out to play with Zrinka's curls. He tried to put a string of her curls in his mouth, but Zrinka quickly pulled them away him.

Beth stood on the other side of the wall, striving to pull apart Zrinka's words. "But how? How is this possible? I mean…" She began pacing along the wall. "If I don't do anything, the job doesn't get done. It just doesn't." She waved her hands in the air. "God does so much. Why should I expect him to do the things that he has asked me to do?"

Zrinka's gaze rested again on Beth. "My dear friend, when God is ask us to do things, we cannot do it, anything, without his help. He give us strength we need. But first we must *ask* him for this strength, this help."

Beth stared at Zrinka's kind brown eyes and the dark shadings beneath them. She reached out and touched her friend's face, realizing that she had not noticed how very tired Zrinka appeared. Looking down at Bruce, Beth softly asked, "Do you ask God for help with Tihomir?"

Zrinka's smile faded slightly from her face. She murmured, "Every day."

~~~

2000: Marko

Marko tried to concentrate as *Gospoda* Filipovic explained something about multiplication. She was waving her arms about, as she often did, emphasizing each aspect of what she was saying. It was as if she actually *cared* about what she was teaching them, which Marko thought ridiculous. After all, what could be interesting about multiplication? There had been times in the past month when her crazy enthusiasm seemed to affect his thinking, and without realizing it, he began to take interest in uninteresting things.

She was tricky that way.

When she had finished explaining the concept, she described the homework for that day and which page it was on. She asked if they had any questions, and, after answering a few, she announced the five minute break. Marko watched as the rows of desk turned into chaos: kids turning to one another to talk, girls giggling, guys laughing, all of their loud voices filling the room. He peeked over at Maggie. Unlike the others, she was sitting quietly and writing something in a workbook. She couldn't be… He turned his head and leaned in to see. She was doing the math homework! He grabbed the workbook from her.

"Hey, give that back." Turning toward him, she tried to take it from his hands.

He ignored her and began erasing everything she had done. She yelled at him to stop and kept trying to grab it from him. When he set it back down on her side of the desk, she stared at him and looked like she was going to cry.

He asked her, "How could you be here for four years and not know that you can't do homework at school?"

She glanced down at her notebook and then back at him with scrunched up eyebrows. "I never thought to do homework here before, but I was thinking how I have a friend coming over after school, and I don't want to have to do homework later on."

He shook his head. "You silly girl. *Home*work is for *home*."

She sat up straighter and stuck her chin up a bit. "Well, it's not like there's a rule or anything. What would it hurt if I did my homework here?"

Sighing, he leaned forward. "Listen, I know kids in other classes who have tried to do homework at school, and the teacher just crosses it all out with a red pen."

She glared at him. "Better than erasing it all. At least with a red mark, I can still see it all to copy it later." She peered at her workbook, as if to try to make out the erased markings.

He muttered under his breath, "Heathens."

She turned back to him. "What did you call me?"

"A heathen."

She paused, her forehead wrinkled. "What does that mean?"

Crossing his arms, he tried to think. He didn't want to admit to her that he didn't know. "It's what my mom calls you and your family."

Her face seemed to soften from being all scrunched up. "Why?"

"Well, you don't come to mass. Except that one time." He tried to think of what else he had heard. "My mom says you don't pray to Mary. And that you probably don't even celebrate Christmas."

Maggie's laugh surprised him. She sat there, looking at him like he had turned into St. Nicholas himself. "Of course we celebrate Christmas!"

"You do?"

She was smiling at him in that way that made him feel like a small child. She nodded. "Yes, we do, every year, every December, and we give each other presents just like you do."

He tried to think of some other questions. "Do you make your own manger like we do?"

"No, but we brought one from America when we first came. We use the same one every year instead of making one each year."

Well, that didn't seem like such a horrible thing. "Why don't you come to mass?"

Maggie set her elbow on the desk and settled her chin in the palm of her hand. Shrugging her shoulders, she answered, "I guess because we have our own mass somewhere else in our own church."

Marko played with his eraser, twisting it about. "You go to church?"

Again, she nodded. "Every Sunday."

The Americans had different ways of going about things, but, in the end, they did not seem to be all that different. He thought of another question and leaned forward. "What about Mary? Do you pray to her?"

Tilting her head, she looked at him. "Why would we pray to Mary when we can pray to Jesus himself?"

Gospoda Filipovic clapped her hands to get everyone's attention. The break was over, and all the kids began returning to their seats. As *Gospoda* Filipovic turned to grammar next, Marko tried again to focus on what was the she was saying, but he was thinking about what the word heathen really meant.

~~~

1993: Tihomir

Tihomir opened the door. "Hello, brother, come in." He embraced Drew in a hug and then motioned him to sit down in the living room. "Zrinka is in our room. She is still not feeling well."

Drew sat down and stared at the closed door to the bedroom. "I'm sorry to hear that." He turned to Tihomir. "We've been worried about her, praying for her, and wondering if there is anything we can do."

Tihomir came over to sit across from Drew in his favorite chair. "She will be *okej*. She is strong and always comes out of it doing well." He smiled and leaned back into the chair.

Studying his own hands, Drew simply nodded.

Tihomir asked him, "Is something troubling you?"

Nodding again, Drew cleared his throat. "Yes, I came to talk to you about something."

Leaning forward, Tihomir scrunched up his eyebrows. "What is it? Something with Beth?"

Drew shook his head. "No, no, she's fine. It's not about us." He too leaned forward, interlacing his hands and then unlacing them. "I want to talk about the sermon on Sunday."

Tihomir leaned back. "What about it?"

Drew stood up and crossed the room. "You spoke on a great passage of Scripture and highlighted some key points. I enjoyed what you said about unity, about all of us working together."

With a laugh, Tihomir leaned back further and crossed one leg over the other. "Well, my friend, that does not sound like such a problem."

Facing the window, Drew gazed out, his eyes seeming to search for something. "I enjoyed it, but it seemed like something was missing."

"Missing?"

Silence filled the space between them as Tihomir wondered what Drew was talking about. He tried to think of a point he had forgotten to mention or an aspect he had overlooked. His sermon had been short, but that's what they had agreed upon beforehand, turning more of the service over to Tanja and Luka so that the two could lead the congregation in worship and prayer.

Drew turned and faced Tihomir. "My friend, you didn't once mention God."

Tihomir stared straight back. "A person can talk about God without specifically mentioning his name."

Drew's gaze remained steady. "You seemed to skip over any verses that mentioned his name."

Tihomir combed his fingers through his hair. "What is your point, Drew?"

Drew crossed the room and sat down again. "Is something going on? Is something wrong?" He leaned forward, concern in his eyes. "You seem to be acting different lately. Like something's changed. And it's been awhile since we prayed together or read the Bible or anything."

"Do I have to be the one to initiate such things all the time?"

"No. Of course not. And I realize that I need to initiate more. I'm just saying that you seem distant. I've had this strange feeling ever since our church outing at Plitvice."

Now Tihomir stood up. "You are the one who has been acting 'different' since that outing."

"Tiho, I don't mean this to sound…"

Tihomir interrupted him, "I mean, you come into my house, and you challenge my authority, my sermon. This is not why I asked you to come to Croatia."

Drew looked up at him. "Why did you ask me to come?" His gaze was penetrating, too intense. Tihomir looked away, and Drew continued, "I thought we were supposed to be partners in this, encouraging and challenging each other."

Tihomir walked toward the kitchen with his back to Drew. "I will ask

Drew stood up and followed him, "Brother, I just want to say…"

Tihomir opened the refrigerator and took out some tomatoes and cucumbers for salad. "I am sorry, Drew, but I need to make lunch for Zrinka and me. Thank you for coming by."

"But…"

"Thank you for coming by."

Drew let his hands hang to his sides and stood there awkwardly for a moment as Tihomir got out a cutting board and a bowl. Finally Drew walked out of the house and shut the door behind him.

Tihomir washed the vegetables and then began to chop them and scrape them into the bowl. Then he remembered the soup and grabbed it from the refrigerator. Opening the container, he spooned it into a small pot, placed the pot on the stove, and turned on one of the burners. Zrinka's mother had brought the soup over earlier that day since she knew that he was not the best cook. After he finished the salad, he began to cut a few slices of bread. Holding the loaf with his left hand, he cut with his right. "How dare he…" He cut one slice. "How could he challenge my authority, my preaching…" Another slice. "His Croatian isn't even that good, so how could he know if…" And another. "He's younger and foreign and doesn't know all that I know…"

He didn't watch where his left thumb was, and he grazed it with the knife. Swearing, he quickly placed his finger under cold water from the sink. He had barely opened the skin, but he noticed then that both of his hands were shaking. Shutting the water off, he slid down against the kitchen cabinets and onto the tile floor. He stared at his shaking hands, water dripping off the tips of his fingers. "It was a good sermon. It was." He made his hands into fists. "I will preach about God… Yes, I will preach about God when He starts showing up in my life." Looking down, he watched as a little bit of blood trickled from his thumb.

XVII

2000: Marko

Marko kicked a can around on the ground, back and forth between his feet. That is, until an old woman yelled at him to "stop that noise." He apologized and leaned against the glass of the bus stop. He could have sat down on one of the blue seats, like the old woman, but he was too excited to sit down. He had just finished his last exam! It had taken him three tries, but, at long last, he had passed it. He could not believe that he was done with his fourth year of high school for economics. After years of working hard and studying as if books were his very food, it seemed as if real life was about to begin.

His eyes alert, he kept searching for Maggie. She was supposed to meet him at this bus stop when she had finished. It was her second time taking this last exam for art, and he was nervous for her. He hoped that she could pass and be done; then they could both celebrate together.

A bus came to a stop in front of him, and the old woman hobbled onto it, mumbling something about young people making too much noise. Her comment made him smile.

Dressed all in black, the widow reminded him of Baka. With all her smoking and coughing, Baka seemed like she could go up to heaven at any moment, but still she held on strong, shaking a finger at anyone who tried to help her too much.

"Boo."

Startled, Marko swung to his left and saw a grinning Maggie. She just stood there, and he looked expectantly at her, waiting for her to speak.

She giggled. "I passed!"

Yelping for joy, he swooped her up and swung her around until she demanded that he let her go. Setting her down, he grinned widely at her.

Maggie rolled her eyes at him and then looked down at her watch.

He looked down the road. "No, it should be here any second."

Plopping her bag down on a blue seat, Maggie sat in the one next to it, closed her eyes, blew up her cheeks, and then let the air escape from her mouth. Marko remained standing, watching her, and shaking his head at her. Oftentimes when she did this, he would comment that she looked like one of those puffer fish. When they were around thirteen, they had watched the movie *Finding Nemo*, and Marko had pointed to the fish that blew up so big when he got angry. "That's you, Maggie."

She hadn't thought it was as funny as he did, which was not unusual since he often said things she didn't approve of. She would usually punch him in the shoulder and scrunch up her face so he knew she was not to be teased. His laughter could hardly be contained, so he often went home with a bruised shoulder.

The bus pulled up to where they were standing. Maggie grabbed her bag and followed Marko onto the bus. Since the bus was packed, the two of them had to stand and hold onto one of the bars above them. Wiping the sweat off her forehead, Maggie spoke loudly over the noise of the bus and the people talking: "Man, it's hot in here." She fanned herself with her hand and then looked over at Marko. "Couldn't we open a window?"

He rolled his eyes at her. "You Americans always want cold air on you. Have you not learned better by now? You'll get sick."

Now it was her turn to roll her eyes. "My mom's a nurse, so I think she would tell me if something would make me sick."

Gritting his teeth kept him from starting another argument with her. They had been friends for years, and arguing continued to be a given with them. Let her think what she wanted. She just did not understand some things.

After a couple minutes, she pointed to his bag. "You got any food in there?"

He shook his head at her. "Maggie, how are you always hungry?"

She put a hand on her hip. "You always have some kind of sandwich."

He gave her a knowing look. "That's because I know I will have to feed you at some point."

Digging around in his backpack, he pulled out a small, paper bag and handed her half of the ham sandwich Mama had made him that morning. How Maggie could eat so much and stay so little was a mystery to everyone. Her family and friends were ever teasing her since she seemed to always be eating something. It was for this reason, and others, that

Mama adored her. Mama loved when Maggie came over to the house because the girl would eat anything that was put in front of her.

Taking a large bite of the sandwich, Maggie smiled with her cheeks full. After she swallowed, she said, "My favorite kind of bread."

As the bus curved around a corner, he shifted his feet and hung on to a bar above his head. "Mama won't buy anything but *crna peka*. She makes me go buy a loaf as soon as I get up in the morning. She likes to make sure they don't run out of it before I get there."

She looked intently at the bread in her hand. "Will you only make this kind of bread when you open your own bakery?"

"If I was only feeding myself. Other people like variety, different kinds of breads..." He winked at her. "Not everyone is as smart as us."

She gazed out the window at the apartments and shops they passed by. "Will you make strudels?"

"Yes."

"And doughnuts?"

"Of course."

Now she looked up at him with raised eyebrows. "With chocolate in the middle?"

He grinned. "What else?"

She took another bite and spoke with her mouth full. "I'll be there every day."

The bus moved around another corner, and Marko tried to steady himself. He looked down at Maggie. Eating the last few bites of his sandwich, she seemed to be ignoring the fact that she would soon be on a plane back to America. "Goodbye" was coming fast.

~ ~ ~

2008, Thursday: Tihomir

Tihomir held the pencil's tip on the paper. The sheet was covered with those annoyingly tiny pieces of eraser. He drew another few lines and then shaded around them. They just weren't right. With the eraser, he blotted it all out again. After another attempt, he finally stood up from his chair and walked over to the bookcase. Pulling out a photo album, he searched for the scene he pictured in his mind: the trees reaching up and the water crashing down. He could feel the mist on his face and hear the roar in his ears, but he couldn't seem to capture the flow and power onto a piece of paper. Flipping to a picture that came close to what he envisioned, he slid it out of its sleeve. He sat down to begin copying that picture and had only been working on it for a few minutes when the phone rang.

"Zrinka?" He waited, yelled her name again, and then heard her open their bedroom door. As he held the picture at arm's length and then up close to his face, he heard Zrinka cough hard and then pick up the phone and begin talking. It was probably someone from his congregation. Many people called with problems they had and asked him for advice.

"Tihomir."

Zrinka was standing in the doorway to the living room with one hand holding the phone and the other covering up the mouthpiece. As he stood up to take the phone from her, he noticed that her eyes were filled and about to spill over; her chin was trembling. He walked over and came to stand in front of her. With his thumb, he wiped away a loose tear from her cheek and whispered, "What's wrong?"

She shook her head and let out a soft cry as well as a cough. Then she kissed his cheek and handed him the phone. "It's your mother."

As he pressed his ear against the phone, he held his wife close to him. Panic streamed through his body like the waterfall he had been trying to draw. Mama's voice filled his ear; she too was crying. He tried to understand her words, tried to calm her down with words of comfort, and then tried not to understand her because he didn't really want to know what could cause these two women of his to cry—these strong women who hardly ever cried.

Holding tightly onto Zrinka, he tried once more to speak. "Mama, what happened? I don't understand."

Her words came through clearly this time. When he didn't respond, Mama repeated the words. He just stood there. Zrinka lifted her head and looked up at him with red eyes. His father's eyes had often been red, never of course because of crying since, after all, real men never cried. No, the old man's eyes had been red after a long afternoon or evening at the bar. When Tihomir would see those eyes of fire, he would leave the house, run in the dark down to the Drava River, and call to God for help, for answers. Now he looked down at Zrinka who was looking up at him, waiting for a response.

He hung up the phone, let go of his wife, and walked back to his drawing pad. Picking it up, he began studying the picture again.

Of course she could not maintain her distance but had to come over to him. She had to kneel at his feet and put her hands on his knees. She had to look up at him with those red eyes.

He murmured, "Leave me alone."

The red eyes blinked. "Tihomir... I... I can't imagine what you must be feeling. It's a... What a tragedy..."

He picked up his pencil. "No tragedy. Nothing to imagine."

Another blink. "Tihomir... your father is dead."

Looking at the picture, he drew the general outline. "So is my sister."

She traced his knees with her fingers and began hesitantly. "I know you have been angry at your father for Ana's death, for his cruelty, and for his hypocrisy, and you have every right. But it's possible and acceptable to be angry at him and upset and still mourn his death."

He focused on his drawing. "Leave me alone."

She gazed up at him, her forehead wrinkled with concern. "You hung up on your mother while she was crying hysterically. This... this just isn't like you."

His eyes remained steady on the white paper and the black lines. "I want to draw this picture."

From her eyes fell droplets. They landed on his knees and darkened his jeans. Though soft, they pierced. She whispered, almost groaned, "Where are you, Tiho? Where is my husband?"

With his right hand, he slapped her hard. And then slapped her again. "I said to leave me alone." He turned back toward his drawing and picked up his pencil once more. "My father is dead, so there is no need to mention him again."

He tried to ignore her, but she just sat there, staring up at him, her presence seeking to penetrate him, but he remained strong and unmovable. After a few moments, she stood up slowly and walked back to the bedroom. He tried not to listen to her cough, a cough that probably crumbled her to her knees. He also tried not to notice how as he put the pencil's tip to the paper, his fingers were trembling.

~~~

2008, Thursday: Beth

Beth heard the door slam. In came Bruce with a grin on his face.

"Hi, Mom."

With one eyebrow raised, Beth folded the shirt she was holding. "Could you find a louder way to shut the door?"

He picked through the bowl on the kitchen table until he found an apple. Setting his teeth into it, he talked with his mouth full. "I'm sure I could."

She added the shirt to the pile of clothes on the couch and stood up to give him a hug. His arms were wide open to engulf her when she shrank back. "Oh, Bruce, you're drenched."

These days Bruce always seemed to be continually bathed in sweat. Nearly every day after school he played football with the other boys, running back and forth on the cement court. She had seen him play, and while he wasn't the best player on the team, he was the most energetic and lively. His passion and excitement for the game seemed to fuel the others.

She turned back to fold the rest of the clothes. "Go take a shower."

He came closer to her with that silly grin on his face. "But I want a hug."

Holding up her hand in front of her, she said, "Bruce Elijah Austin, if you touch me, you're folding your own clothes, you understand me?"

At that, he threw his arms up in response, retreated, and bounced away to the bathroom.

While folding the last pair for pants, Beth remembered that she had another load in the washing machine that she needed to hang up. "Wait, Bruce!" She grabbed the empty laundry basket beside her, went to the already closed bathroom door, and knocked.

He opened the door. "Now, you want a hug?"

"No, stop that. I need to get another load of laundry from the washing machine." She looked around. "And how can you be in here so quick? Did you get clean underwear?"

He rolled his eyes. "Oh come on, Mom. I'm *twelve* years old."

Bending down, she reached into the machine and began to pull out the wet heap out and toss it into the basket. "Exactly. Twelve year old boys often forget the important things in life, like cleanliness."

With a dramatic sigh, he headed out of the bathroom. She heard him fumbling about his room. Looking around inside the washing machine, she checked to make sure she had not missed any socks. She yelled out, "There's clean underwear in your pile on the couch."

She heard him clomp into the living room. The boy always sounded like a herd of elephants. Once she had tried to teach him how to walk gently and quietly up and down the hallway. The lesson had not lasted more than a minute before he began acting like a ballerina and trying to twirl around. He had goofed off and laughed and laughed until she threw her hands up in the air and gave up on him.

Boys.

Hoisting the basket onto her right hip, she walked past Bruce as he waved his underwear at her. She just shook her head at him and walked outside onto the balcony. Taking the first pair of shorts, she hung it up with two clothespins on the clothesline. When she had first moved to Croatia, she had complained about the lack of a nice, big dryer. Especially in the winter, the clothes took several hours to dry, and the wind sometimes blew clothes into the landlord's garden. But since they had moved to the new apartment, which was only a few blocks away from the old one, she had begun to think of doing the laundry as a treat. At the new apartment, she could hang her laundry on the balcony, and over the years, it had become a sort of haven to her. A place where she could talk to God, sometimes venting out her anger and sometimes whispering prayers for Drew, the children, herself, or someone she knew who was in need. Whenever she was feeling upset or helpless, she needed something to do with her hands. Hanging up the laundry gave her body something to do while her mind and heart processed.

As she hung up one of Drew's shirts, she heard the phone ring inside. Pinning the shirt in place, she went back into the house and picked up the phone in the kitchen. "Hello?"

She didn't hear anything on the other end. "Hello?"

Something that sounded like a sob came from the phone.

Usually she waited for the other person to talk so that she would know whether to speak in English or Croatian. She waited another moment. Then, taking a deep breath, she said in Croatian, "Whoever you are, whatever is going on, you can tell me."

"Beth, it is Zrinka."

Beth sat down on one of the kitchen chairs. She had not heard from Zrinka in years. She lived only a few blocks away, so their paths often crossed: in the street, at the bakery… Although they had tried to get together or at least talk on the phone, Tihomir had made it harder and harder to do until, lately, when Beth would try to call, she would hear only one ring after another. With a hard swallow, Beth said, "I've never stopped praying for you."

"Nor I for you."

Beth paused, trying to think. She smoothed the wrinkles out of her jeans by pressing her palm against them. Then she asked, "Is something wrong?"

Silence. Heavy silence.

She waited.

Then came a faint plea. "I need to talk to you. May I come to your house?"

"Of course, but Tihomir…"

Urgency surged through the phone receiver. "Please, Beth, I need you to come pick me up. Tihomir is gone right now. Please?"

"I'll be right there."

XVIII

2008, Thursday: Marko

"It is hot," Marko said as he wiped some sweat off his cheek. The bus ride had been suffocating as more people poured in, and there was little air. He would never say it out loud, but he began to wonder if Maggie was right about opening the windows. It sure would help cool off the passengers. And how could one get sick if it was like thirty-something degrees Celsius? Even now, after getting off the bus, he and Maggie succumbed to the sun piercing down on them. Usually a soft wind would come and ease the heat, but today was uncharacteristically hot.

"You want to go for a swim later?" Maggie asked as she huffed away next to him. Unfortunately, the bus stop was at the bottom of the hill they lived on. While Maggie said it kept them fit, Marko would personally have preferred to keep fit by kicking a ball around.

"Yes, swimming sounds good." The sea would be pretty warm from the heat, but it would be a relief nonetheless.

Since Maggie's house was the closest, they stopped there for a drink and a break for Marko before he continued up the hill to his house. As they entered her apartment, they looked at each other, both seeming to have remembered that they had just finished high school. They grinned and ran inside, throwing down their backpacks in the hallway. Maggie yelled out, "I'm done! I'm done!"

Bruce came out of his room. With his finger to his lips, he shushed them.

Maggie didn't pay attention. Running up to Bruce, she said, "I passed the exam. I'm all done!"

Bruce tried again. "Maggie, you're so loud. Be quiet."

Seeing her hands go to her hips, Marko knew Maggie did not like to be told what to do, especially by Bruce.

"Be quiet? Don't you tell me to be quiet."

Bruce shook his head. "Just because you're the oldest..."

Maggie turned her back to him and rolled her eyes at Marko.

"Listen, Maggie." Bruce looked behind him. "Zrinka's here."

Marko was trying to think of who Zrinka was, but he saw on Maggie's face a mixture of joy and wonder. She began to look around and venture back to the rest of the apartment.

Bruce blocked her way.

"You're being annoying." Maggie tried to push him aside.

"Maggie, listen. Mom left with the car, didn't tell me where she was going, and came back with Zrinka... who was crying." He motioned outside. "She and Mom are out on the balcony, talking, and they've been out there for an hour." He looked out to where the two women sat and then looked back to Maggie. "Something's wrong."

Maggie once again had her hands on her hips, but this time her eyes were to the ground, and she was biting down on her lower lip, which meant she was thinking hard. When she lifted her head, she turned and looked at Marko. "I'm sorry, but I think you'd better go."

"*Okej.*" Marko picked up his backpack, which he had flung on the floor when they had entered. He wished he could get a drink of water before he left, but he saw the concern in Maggie's eyes. "We'll see each other later."

She nodded.

He turned away and walked out the door, closing it behind him. For a moment, he stood there, the sun piercing his face. Going inside seemed to have made the heat only worse. There was a summer when he was little when it was so hot that his dad took him to the beach every afternoon. They would run down to the shore and into the water, seeing who could splash the other the most. It was that summer that he had learned how to swim. His dad had been a patient teacher, showing Marko how to breathe properly and how to make his strokes just right. Every summer afterward, Marko would spend most of his time in the water and was able to out swim any boy or girl.

He leaned against the door and kicked a loose rock, watching it fumble down the driveway. It didn't look like Maggie would be able to go swimming with him that afternoon. How he hated seeing her worried and concerned. Closing his eyes, he wondered about many things.

But mostly he wondered if the son of Mary could truly hear his prayers.

~~~

2008, Thursday: Beth

Beth allowed Drew to lead her out the door. His hand tugged onto hers, and she followed him into the lamp-lit street. As no one was out driving this late, the two walked side-by-side down the middle of the road. Many of the houses still had lights on, and Beth listened to the voices of people talking, yelling, and laughing. Croatians stayed up late, even the little ones, and then would have a nice, long nap the next afternoon. She smiled as she thought of what a struggle it had been to get Maggie and Bruce to go to bed at a "normal" time when they were little.

Beth peered over at Drew. "You think Zrinka will be OK?" She asked, rubbing Drew's thumb with hers.

"Tonight?" he gazed up at the curved half-moon and then nodded. "Yes, Maggie seems to be cheering her up. I thought your movie suggestion was a good idea."

Beth nodded. "After our long talk today, she just needed to take her mind of things for a while."

Drew looked down at their hands. "But the question is what next."

"Yes."

With his free hand, he rubbed at his eyes. His allergies seemed to be getting to him. Usually he only battled allergies during the spring and fall, but this summer his eyes seemed to be constantly driving him nuts. He shook his head. "It doesn't seem like the greatest timing. What with us leaving so soon and all."

She gazed down the street, as far as she could see to the bakery at the corner. "It's hard to believe."

He shuffled his feet. "Three more days."

She was not much of a crier, yet now her throat closed up, and she struggled to push the gulf down. She could tell that Drew had noticed by the way he wrapped his arm around her waist and drew her closer to him. She murmured to him, "I never thought this place would become home."

He hung his head. There was a hint of mischief in his voice as he said, "What am I going to do without my fresh bread every day."

Beth laughed at his forlorn face. It reminded her of Bruce when he was five years old and had been chastised for taking his finger around the edge of the chocolate cake and then licking the icing off his finger. His face had gone from ultimate delight to sorrowful and despairing at the thought of "no more." Drew looked much the same now. Every morning he walked to the end of their street and bought a fresh loaf of *crna peka*. It reminded her of the French baguette in that it was crunchy on the outside and soft on the inside, only it was darker than white bread. It also wasn't like the dense rye bread of Germany. Nor did it have the taste of wheat bread or any kinds of seeds or grains.

She grinned up at him. "Maybe we could get you a bread maker."

He scrunched up his face and looked at her as if she had suggested that he take up knitting. Then he sighed dramatically. "I *suppose* if it's the only way I can get fresh bread." He kicked a rock down the road, and the silliness faded from his face. "I remember walking past some bakeries in Sacramento. Might be worth looking into."

They walked in silence for a while. Drew continued to kick a rock around as if it were a soccer ball, back and forth between his feet. Beth thought of all that they needed to pack and remembered the six suitcases they had brought from California back in 1993. They had accumulated a lot since then. At least this time she had two children who could pack their own stuff and help out with the rest. She thought of gifts she had received over the years— like the rug in the living room and the lamp in their bedroom—gifts that wouldn't fit into suitcases and would have to be given away.

Drew released her for a moment to take out a tissue from his pocket. He blew his nose loud enough for everyone in the neighborhood to hear, and she wondered if his allergies would bother him as much in California. It had been so long that she couldn't remember if he had had allergies before they came to Croatia. She was about to ask him when he said, "I think I'm going to go see Tihomir tomorrow."

She glanced over at him. "You are?"

He nodded.

"I mean…" She bit on her lower lip. "You think he'd even let you in the house?"

Drew's eyes were steady, set on the road ahead of them. "I have to try."

~~~

2008: Friday, Tihomir

Tihomir stirred the tomato soup. After setting down the long, wooden spoon, he opened a cabinet. How could there be no basil? He felt like he had just bought some a few days ago. Ever since Zrinka had gotten weaker and become sick more often, he had taken over most of the cooking and grocery shopping. Not that he minded much. He begun to realize that he enjoyed cooking, experimenting to see what tasted good, and making food look artistic like he would with a drawing. The issue he had with it was how much time and energy it took. He could not understand how Zrinka had managed it all on her own, and he just wished he could have her help here and there.

Where was she?

Yesterday he had gone out to buy her flowers—daisies to brighten up her room. Although she enjoyed petunias and begonias, daisies were definitely her favorite kind of flower. She had worn them in her hair in their wedding, and she often decorated the house with them. He had bought the flowers with the hope that such a gift would help smooth over what he had done. Throughout their twenty-one years of marriage, he had never hit her like that, had never hit anyone in his life, and he never would again. His father's death had just come as a shock, and sometimes she said things that provoked his anger.

Yesterday when he had come home, he found a vase on the top of the refrigerator, cleaned it out, filled it up with water, and placed the daisies in it. Then he walked to their bedroom, opened the door slowly, and peered into the dark room. She had been sleeping a lot the past few days, so he had kept the blinds closed during the day to keep the light out. As his eyes slowly adjusted to the dark, he walked over to her side of the bed and whispered, "Zrinka?" He set down the flowers on her nightstand and then gently pulled the covers back.

But she wasn't there.

He was frightened and worried as he called out her name and searched the rest of the house and outside. He called her mom, but Zrinka wasn't with her. He ran down the street and around the block, checking at the grocery store in case she had the strength and had gone to get groceries. Then he ran home again to see if she had returned. But no, she was not there. No note as to where she had gone. He noticed that she had taken her cell phone, so he called her over and over, but it kept going straight to voicemail without ringing.

Throughout yesterday and today his emotions kept raging back and forth between worry for her and anger at her for leaving him like this. Where was she? Why would she just leave with no explanation? How could she do this to him? Was she all right? Was she safe?

What if he lost her?

Hearing a knock on the door, he jumped and dropped the spoon into the pot. Swearing, he picked it out and tossed it into the sink. When he ran over to the door, he realized that he expected it to be Zrinka. But of course, it wouldn't be. How stupid of him. She wouldn't knock on the door of her own house.

He opened the door and there stood Drew.

After all those years, the American could not have had worse timing. Tihomir crossed his arms over his chest. "What do you want?"

Drew hesitated and then stepped closer. "I'd like to come in and talk to you."

Tihomir's eyebrows knitted. "What are you up to?"

Drew looked around the yard and cleared his throat. "Tiho... Zrinka's at our house."

Tihomir's arms dropped to his sides. He should have known. Why had he not thought to look there? He had just thought that after all these years, she would have forgotten about those Americans, pushed them out of her heart just as he had done... at least had tried to do. He shook his head. "That's not her place. She should be home with me."

"You really frightened her."

Noticing that his right hand was shaking, Tihomir made a fist to control it. "We had an argument, and now that we have calmed down, we need to talk things through."

Drew was looking directly at him. "That wasn't quite her story."

Tihomir avoided Drew's direct gaze. He focused on the doorframe, noticing a crack. "So you came to criticize me?"

Drew's look softened. "We heard about your father. I'm sorry, friend."

Friend. Yes, that had been what they had called each other. Tihomir laughed. "Why should you be sorry? You met my father. You know what he is... what he was like."

Drew nodded. "Yes, and I know how cruel he was to you. But I'm sure it, his death, still must hurt you."

Tihomir didn't like the way Drew was looking at him. That look of pity. He wasn't some poor refugee child that needed help. "I'm fine."

Drew took a step forward. "He beat you, didn't he?"

Tihomir felt like Drew had punched him. Perhaps in the head because that was where he felt the pressure. That horrible pressure that always escalated when he couldn't control his emotions. His father had always warned him against crying. His father would only hit him more if he did cry. But Tihomir had never been able to stop himself from crying, and so the beatings had never stopped.

Drew put a hand on his shoulder. "You were only a child."

Tihomir shrugged off Drew's hand and took a step back.

But Drew only stepped forward again. "It wasn't your fault that your father beat you. You were a boy. He shouldn't have done what he did to you."

Tihomir raised his hand, pointing a finger at Drew. "Stop it."

Drew continued, "You did nothing to deserve that kind of treatment. You were just a boy."

Tihomir blinked hard and swallowed hard. "I said stop it!"

Drew once again laid his hand on Tihomir's shoulder. "Your father was a pastor who should have been teaching you about the love of God. Instead he taught you that cruelty and violence are the only ways to treat those you love."

Tihomir tried to punch Drew, but the American had grown stronger than him over the years. Drew overpowered him and held his arms down. Tihomir resisted against him, but Drew's hold on him was strong, and Tihomir soon found himself on the floor of his hallway, trying to break free. He shook his head. "God doesn't love me!"

Drew's voice was quiet but strong. "Yes, he does. He loves you, Tiho."

Tihomir kept fighting against Drew, trying to free his hands. "I'm a man who beats his wife with his words and now with his fists. I don't know how to love, and I don't deserve to be loved."

Drew held him by the arms tightly with his eyes piercing Tihomir. "God loves you, and so do I."

"No." Tihomir shook his head. "You hate me. I turned the whole church against you." Then Tihomir looked up at Drew. "What's wrong with you? Don't you remember? I brought you into the church that day. I kicked you and your family out. I had all the leaders go around the room. I had them criticize you. I had them say what they thought was wrong with you."

"Yes, you did." For a moment, Tihomir saw pain in the American's eyes, a heavy pain. Then Drew breathed in deeply. "But I still prayed for you, every time you came to mind."

Tihomir shook his head hard. "Why? Why would you do that?"

"Because." Tihomir could see the struggle in Drew's eyes, the struggle to say what he was saying. Drew continued, "Because you're my friend. You're my brother."

Tihomir twisted himself, trying to break free from Drew's hold on him, trying not to listen to the American's words. He wished Drew would just leave.

Drew's voice was raw as he continued, "I forgave you that day you kicked us out, and I've forgiven you every day since."

"No, no, that's… It's…" Tihomir couldn't understand. He couldn't accept it.

Drew let go of Tihomir's arms and clamped strongly down on Tihomir's shoulders. Drew's voice and eyes held a deep intensity. "You were my brother then, and you are my brother now. Don't you see? Your father was not the father a boy should have growing up. And, in fact, no earthly father can be what we need. God alone is our real father, and in him, you and I will always be brothers."

Tihomir grabbed hold of Drew's arms, clenched tightly, wanting to smash Drew to pieces, wanting the American to feel the anguish Tihomir was feeling right then. Did he not realize how these words gripped Tihomir's heart and twisted it to breaking? He wanted to hit the man before him, but somehow he couldn't. Instead, he let go of his tight hold and fell against Drew. He began to sob—a deep, ugly cry that came from the darkest parts of him. He held onto this man he had despised and disdained, and he held onto him like he was his one and only chance at survival. And Drew just sat there, letting him cry, saying over and over, "My brother. My brother."

XIX

2008, Friday: Beth

Beth wrapped another box up tightly with tape. She would have thought that by now she would have the process down to a fine art, but she was still clumsy with tearing the tape. She still struggled to place it properly onto the gap where the two sides came together. And she still struggled with the fact that this home would soon be nothing more than an empty apartment.

"Where's dad?" Maggie asked.

Beth glanced out into the hallway. Zrinka was resting on the couch in the living room. Standing up from the bed, Beth picked up an empty box from the floor. She began taking books down from Maggie's shelves. "He went to see Tihomir."

Maggie slowly stood up to help Beth with the books. "It's been a long time since we've seen him."

"Yes. Yes, it has."

Kneeling next to her, Maggie began to take books off the lower shelves. "I mean, we *see* him, but... you know."

Beth nodded.

Placing a handful of books into the box, Maggie looked down at them. "Mom, how am I going to pack when we get to the States? I mean, how do I decide what to take to college? I feel like I have a lot of stuff."

Beth shook her head. "You don't have that much, Maggs. I bet you'll have a roommate with twice as much." She reached for some tape to seal up the box. "The thing you need to think about now is what to do with all your drawings you have here."

"Well, I've chosen the ones I want to take with me." Maggie looked up at the four walls that were covered with sketches, charcoal drawings, and watercolor paintings. "I've also been thinking about giving some of them away as gifts."

When Maggie fell silent, Beth looked up and saw that her daughter's eyes were turning red. She could tell that Maggie was trying to fight it. Beth drew her into her arms. "It's OK, Maggs." She held her and rocked her tightly. "This is a tough time. It's OK to cry."

Maggie shook her head. "I don't know how I'm going to say goodbye to everyone."

Beth reached for some tissues and handed them to Maggie. "Bruce told me that Marko walked you home yesterday and then left when you heard about Zrinka."

"He's my best friend." Maggie gazed around at the various boxes that littered the wood floor. "I can't imagine not seeing him every day. Drawing with him. Talking with him. "

Maggie shifted and lay down so her head was in Beth's lap. Beginning to comb Maggie's hair with her fingers, Beth let the girl cry while she thought about the goodbyes she herself would have to be making soon.

Fifteen years of ministry and friendships and life. Their small home group had slowly grown into numbers that their house could no longer hold, so they had moved the "church" downtown to an old theater they rented. Over the years, Beth had developed strong relationships with the women in the church, and together they had started a women's Bible study and prayer group. She had even started the process of getting over her insecurities and had helped lead worship.

Stroking Maggie's hair, she thought of how her daughter would soon be going off to college. In a way, she felt like she was about to lose her. Maggie wouldn't be around as much and would be busy with university life. And in leaving Croatia, Beth was also leaving behind all the memories, or rather, reminders of memories, of Maggie's childhood. Beth looked around the room and then out the window to the garden. Both of her children had grown up here.

And that's when it hit Beth. She couldn't identify a specific moment, but somewhere in the midst of the stress of ministry, the ups and downs of parenting, and the constant struggle with the language, this place had become home.

And California now seemed like some far off, unknown, foreign place.

Beth murmured, "Maggie." She brushed the girl's curls off her face.

Maggie slowly sat up, her eyes puffy.

With the back of her fingers, Beth wiped away the tears on her daughter's cheeks. "Let's leave these books for now. There's some place I want to go."

Standing up, Beth offered her hand and helped pull Maggie up. The two walked out to the living room, and Beth explained to Zrinka that they would return in a bit. Then, sliding into their flip-flops, they shuffled out the door. There was a subtle breeze that played with both mother and daughter's curls. They walked down the hill and crossed the street to the *pazar* as they immersed themselves in the wild dance of color—fresh fruit, football jerseys, souvenirs of all different sizes and interests… The old men and women laid out their display of products on gray slabs of cement, calling out to the quick-paced tourists of all different nationalities. The tourists who were bent on entitlement and customer service were often met with grumpy expressions and gruff responses. But Beth had learned that those wrinkled faces would become enveloped in smiles if but offered a kind word and a minute or two of conversation.

As the two of them entered deeper into this living chaos, they curved toward the left to the vegetable stands. And there he was: *Barba* Goran. His lips were arched down in a frown as he dealt with a large woman who could not seem to make up her mind as to how many heads of lettuce she wanted. Shaking his head, finally, *Barba* Goran threw two heads of lettuce into a bag, tossed it onto the scale, and then named his price. The woman looked up at him, shocked, and then handed him a wad of bills, which clearly stated, "I am a tourist who has no idea what these colorful papers are worth, so I give them all to you, hoping you're an honest man."

Lucky for her, he was. He grabbed one of the bills and handed the rest back to her. He then grabbed a few coins from his little fanny pack that he had strapped to his waist and tossed them into her hand. Turning his head, he caught sight of Beth and Maggie, and his face lit up like a Christmas tree. Ignoring another customer who had come to his stand, he beckoned the two women to come over. He shook their hands and kissed them on both cheeks. When the customer tried to get his attention, he continued to ignore the man and invited Beth and Maggie to come sit with him behind the stone slab. He asked them how Bruce was doing—was he becoming the next Davor Suker—how was Drew—was he getting fat off Beth's cooking—and on and on.

The men and women who worked alongside him were always shocked at how Goran radically transformed whenever a member of the crazy American family came over to visit his stand.

After talking for a while, Goran grew serious and laid a hand on Beth's hand. "You have to leave soon, yes?"

Beth nodded. "Yes, in two days."

He patted her hand. "Whenever you come back, you always come for vegetables to me, yes? You don't go anywhere else, *okej*? No one have good vegetables like Goran." He smiled his wide, toothless grin.

"I wouldn't think of buying them anywhere else." It was her turn to pat his hand. "Thank you for your kindness over the years, your warmth, and all the delicious vegetables you shared with us." She shook her head. "I'll never forget it."

He waved off her compliments, undoubtedly embarrassed. He offered the typical "it's nothing," and then snapped at a woman who tried to ask him a question about his potatoes. He waved the woman away and yelled to his left, "Čićo, help this woman. I'm busy!"

Then he turned to Maggie, took her hands in his thick, leathery hands and kissed hers gently. "*Princesa moja*, my garden will miss you very much. It will be very sad to see you leave. So you must come back soon, yes?" When she nodded, he smiled. Then he turned to his bag, took out one pink rose, and handed it to her. "The roses, they wait for you because... they do not like my face so much. You see all these wrinkles?" He pointed to his face and laughed. "But your face—" He paused as a soft smile covered his lips. "*Princesa*, your face is like angel."

Maggie lifted the rose up to her face, closed her eyes, and breathed in. Over the years, she had helped *Barba* Goran plant rose bushes at the beginning of every spring. They spent hours tending to the bushes, making sure they were well taken care of. Beth loved going over to his house with Maggie, standing off to the side, and watching the two of them in his garden as he taught her everything she needed to know about plants and vegetables.

Maggie leaned forward, placed her hand on *Barba* Goran's cheek, and kissed the other. His cheeks grew red, and he was about to say something when Maggie threw her arms around his neck. She murmured to him, "*Volim te, Barba.*"

The old man hugged her back and then let her go, unashamedly allowing the tears to flow down his cheeks. Later on, when Beth would look back on that moment, she would always think of how she had never seen a more beautiful face.

Beth and Maggie stood and said good-bye to him, not before he had, of course, given them both several bags of vegetables. Though they protested profusely, he would hear none of it, waved off their protests, and forced the bags into their hands. Then he shooed them off, telling them that they needed to go home and eat something since they were nothing but skin and bones. The two women laughed, thanked him, and walked away, their arms full, their hearts full, and each of them saying silent goodbyes to the little, seemingly insignificant sights they passed all along the way home.

~~~

2008, Sunday: Tihomir

Tihomir walked alone beside the bank of the Cetina River. He had taken off his flip-flops and allowed the dirt, little blades of grass, and small rocks to make imprints on the soles of his feet. Here he had baptized many people of his church. Here he had led people to the water's edge, immersed them in its breadth, and celebrated with them as they rose up out of it. The river was always much colder than the sea, even in the summer. He dipped his foot into it. Like recently melted ice: freezing, but refreshing. Diving into it often felt like waking up suddenly out of a dream.

Like how he felt now.

His eyes felt puffy and his head hurt from yesterday and the day before. He hadn't cried that hard and that long since Ana had died.

He stepped forward. The cool water splashed lightly against his ankles. Then, fully clothed, he entered into the water as it rose up to his knees, to his waist, and then to his shoulders. Slowly, all of this slowly. He felt the cold pierce every millimeter of his skin, felt the breeze skid across the top of the water and tug on him, calling to him to enter deeper. He listened, and turning around, closed his eyes, leaned back, and submerged himself into the river's depths. He pushed himself down and came to rest near the bottom.

Underneath the water's surface, he heard each word, each cruelty, and each untruth that he had spoke to his wife, to his congregation. He tasted of every manipulation, every pride-filled action. He felt the slaps, the first and then the second, that he had sent across Zrinka's face just three days ago. And then he saw the face of God before him, the one he had spat on and cursed.

He deserved to die.

His lungs burned, but he kept himself there, at the river's depths. This was where a person like him belonged after all, wasn't it? He was a thief—he had stolen joy, rid their house of it, and buried it so as to never find it again. He had not kept the Sabbath day holy but rather had soiled it with his preaching, with his hypocrisy. He had dishonored his father with animosity and judgment. And he had hated his brother, his brother in Christ, with a hatred that savored strongly of murder.

Brother. That had been what Drew had called him, repeating it over and over, like drop after drop of a steady rain. *My brother.*

My son.

Tihomir opened his eyelids, and the water pierced his eyes. Two words, seemingly audible—a name, an identity. And having heard these two words, he pressed his hands onto the bottom of the river and pushed up. As his head burst forth from the water, he gulped in the air. He tossed his head back and choked in breath after breath. Tihomir had never tasted anything so good, so pure. The air was crisp and filled him up with breadth and volume. He gazed up at the tall trees. Like the trees on Marjan, they created a smooth rustling that electrified the air. Once at a baptism, a similar thing had happened, and Zrinka had later commented that it was as if the trees were clapping, applauding a new life.

And here they were again, applauding him, or rather, applauding what God had done.

Tihomir now rose out of the water and walked back to the bank. Turning, he looked out at the water. As a child, he had run down to the Drava River, run to it in the dark looking for answers, sketching alongside its edge, seeking to capture truth. And now, six hundred kilometers south, he had come to the Cetina River, and he had found God. Or rather, God had found him.

My son.

~~~

2008, Monday: Marko

Marko sat on the steps outside his house. Mama would normally be running out to him with a cushion for him to sit on, or at least come out onto the balcony and yell at him. But she seemed to know to leave him alone that day. She had even announced that she would be making *pasticada*, which she only made on special occasions.

It made a guy feel worse when people were being overly nice to him.

In his hand he held the drawing Maggie had given him before she left. It was a scene of the inside of a bakery with a couple of people looking down through the glass at various pastries. Behind the counter stood a grinning version of himself with his arms crossed in front of him. She had made him look proud, like he had swum across the Adriatic Sea all the way to Italy.

Maggie had always encouraged him toward his dream, whether it be playing football, drawing, or owning a bakery. She had been the one to suggest he go to high school for economics.

And now she was gone.

When he had been little, he would often fall and scratch his knees. One time in particular he had fallen down a few stairs in the stairwell. Of course, like a little girl, he began to cry immediately. His father came running out of their apartment and down to where Marko sat. Tata drew Marko into his arms, rocked him, and whispered over and over again. "It is *okej*, son. Cry. Do not hold it in. It is *okej*."

They sat like that for a while, Tata murmuring a few words of comfort, but mostly just holding him. When Marko calmed down, he looked up into Tata's eyes and noticed that they were red and watery. Marko wiped his nose with the back of his hand. "I thought men were not supposed to cry."

Tata looked at him. "A man knows when a time is right to cry. When a man's son is hurting—and that man loves his son very much—then I think that is a time when he should cry."

Now, outside that same apartment, Marko put his head down into his lap and let the sobs come. Tata was not there anymore, and neither was Maggie. And he still was unsure what it meant to have faith like Maggie did, a faith that went beyond mass, beyond rosaries, and beyond prayers to the saints. Maggie was the kind of person who was always talking about Jesus, and, though he had often teased her about it, he wished he could be more like her and know more about this man, this son of God, who was more than a figure on a crucifix. He wanted to know more about this person who apparently, for some reason, wanted a relationship with a young man like Marko.

He was still thinking about all this when he felt something hit his leg.

A soccer ball.

He looked up, and there stood Tomo.

Even though they had not seen each other as much after elementary school, having gone their separate paths for high school, they would still go up to the cement court sometimes and show the little kids how to really play. Then they would stop off at *Barba* Leo's store and buy drinks and snacks just like old times.

With his hands on his hips, Tomo shook his head with a smile. "Come on, Grandma." He motioned for Marko to follow him.

Marko grabbed the ball, bounced it once, twice, and then got up to his feet. He kicked the ball to Tomo, and they shuffled it back and forth between them and down the driveway.

After all, there was a time to cry.

And then there was a time to play some football.

ABOUT THE AUTHOR

Faith Riccomi grew up in Croatia as a missionary kid, much like the character Maggie. She began writing as a way to process her childhood, and subsequently this novel and all of its characters evolved. After years of moving around Europe and the United States, she has settled down in Southern California while maintaining her love of other cultures through short-term missions.

Made in the USA
Middletown, DE
20 March 2022

62746236R00144